THE GHOST OF GRAYDON PLACE

DOROTHY FRANCIS

SCHOLASTIC INC.
New York Toronto London Auckland Sydney

ISBN 0-590-32545-0

15 14 13 12 11 10 9 8 7 6 5   1 2 3 4 5/9

THE GHOST OF GRAYDON PLACE

A Windswept Book

WINDSWEPT TITLES
FROM SCHOLASTIC

• 1 •

Tracy welcomed the touch of Mac's fingers twining through hers, yet she leaned forward in the backseat of the Sterling car so she could see around his broad shoulders, his rangy frame, and get one last look at the Drake campus as Mrs. Sterling braked at a stoplight.

"Sit back," Mac invited, his calm blue eyes regarding her fondly. "Relax. There's plenty of room. If it weren't for these winter clothes . . ." He smoothed his gray flannel slacks and pulled his down jacket closer to his lean body in an attempt to make more space; then he flipped the jacket collar up around his ears until the bronze brown fabric blended with his thick mane of carefully cut hair.

Tracy smiled to herself, admiring Mac as she eased back into the crevice between him and Tom that was barely large enough to accommodate her slim frame. Wide-set eyes. High, broad cheekbones. Full mouth. Mac reminded her of the picture of King Arthur in

1

a storybook that had been her favorite as a child. All day long she had noticed girls turning to give Mac a second glance. But now the campus vied with him for her attention.

"Black and blue." Mac winked, eyeing her dark hair and her skirt and blazer. "My favorite color combination."

She barely heard him. How she wished she would be coming to Des Moines and enrolling at Drake University next year! But she didn't voice her wish; no use risking an argument with Mac in front of Tom and Jill and Jill's mother. She and Mac had had enough discussions about whether or not she should accept an engagement ring for Christmas, about whether or not they should plan to be married right after she was graduated from high school in June. She was in no mood to think about future problems and decisions today, not when everything had been so perfect.

"Hey!" Tom shouted in her left ear and nudged her with his elbow. "It's starting to snow." He had been holding his tan coat in his lap, and now he slipped it on over his green cords and yellow, crew-neck sweater.

"Ta-da!" Mac held his hand to his mouth as if it were a megaphone. "And ace reporter Tom Crendal gives the world another first." Mac lowered his hand. "What would we do without you and your astute observations, Tom?"

"Ha!" Tom raked his fingers through his black hair, leaving it standing in dark, featherlike tufts that contrasted with his

January-pale face. "When I'm a famous journalist working on *The New York Times* or *The Washington Post*, you'll see my byline and say, 'Ah, I knew that boy when he was writing for *Pebbles* at good old Marshalltown High. Always knew Tom would make good.'"

Tracy grinned at Tom's staccato chatter. "Enough, you two." She brushed her hair from her eyes as she grinned at the boys. "This is no time for sarcasm. We all should be congratulating Jill on her number-one rating. You did a *super* job, Jill. I'll bet you were the best flute player those three judges heard all day."

"Sure thing." Tom leaned forward and slapped Jill on the back. "That superior rating along with your being chosen for All State Band should grab you the Tye music scholarship for next year."

Jill half turned where she was sitting in a bucket seat beside her mother. She smiled her thanks as she pulled her white turtleneck sweater up under her chin, buttoned her red blazer, and then reached down to see if the car heater was blowing warm air. "I'm keeping my fingers crossed, gang. No scholarship, no college."

"You'll get it," Tom said. "I'm going to give you a great write-up in *Pebbles*. That should help keep your name in the minds of the people on the scholarship committee."

"I'll probably gain ten more pounds waiting for their decision." Jill sighed. "I wish I'd inherited Mom's metabolism. I gained five pounds from nervous eating, worrying about this contest."

"Maybe you should have inherited my will power," her mother said, laughing. "I'd look like a blimp if I didn't diet."

Tracy glanced at Mrs. Sterling in her gray, tailored coat and suit and she couldn't imagine her looking anything but super sharp. Even her salt-and-pepper hair was chic. Had her hair once been as black as Jill's was now? Tracy smiled at Jill. With their dark hair and creamy complexions, Jill and Tom looked enough alike to be brother and sister, instead of a great couple.

Jill quickly changed the subject from dieting. "Tom, when you write that article, just remember that Tracy deserves a lot of the credit. Without a good accompanist a soloist is down the tubes."

"It was fun playing for you, Jill," Tracy said. She felt Mac squeeze her hand and she smiled at him, pleased that he had chosen to spend his Saturday afternoon with her at the music contest, taking time off from his weekend job as museum guide in Iowa City. She enjoyed playing the piano, but she had no desire to make a career of music-as Jill did. If she went to college she wanted to go into pre-law. If. That was the big word — if.

"It's snowing harder, kids." Mrs. Sterling signaled for a left turn. "I hope . . ." Her voice trailed away as she snapped on the radio. "See if you can tune in a weather report, will you, Jill?"

4

Tracy looked outside where snow was falling in big, wet flakes that were clinging to the windows and were already beginning to pile up at the sides of the freeway. But she wasn't worried. Mrs. Sterling was a good driver. She was always taking a carload of kids somewhere, and she didn't let weather and traffic flap her like some people did. A paper-clip type of person, Tracy thought. Jill's mother is the kind who holds things together.

Mac's presence added to her feeling of well-being. Dependable. Calm. Mac never pushed himself forward, but he could cope with a bad situation when necessity demanded. She always felt good with Mac.

Again Tom nudged Tracy with his elbow. "Look at this. How's this for a headline?"

Tracy read from the yellow notepad Tom was holding. "JILL STERLING IS NUMBER ONE." She grinned, knowing Tom thought Jill was a number one for many reasons. They had been dating since their junior year. It was amazing when she stopped to think about it — Tom with his jumping-jack mind that encouraged leaping before looking, and Jill with her pragmatic, ever-practical bent.

"JILL STERLING IS NUMBER ONE." Mac repeated the potential headline. "Very creative." His resonant bass voice assumed a tone that was half sincere, half teasing.

"Hope it makes the front page, Tom," Tracy said. "You and Jill both deserve a front-page spread." Suddenly Tracy felt very much out of it. Next fall Tom would be going to the University of Missouri to study journalism. Jill was almost certain to be enrolling in music at Drake. Jill was sometimes pessimistic about her chances, but she usually reached her goals. Mac would be a senior in archaeology at the University of Iowa. And Tracy Pendelton? Where would she be? She wished she were two people. Then one of her could marry Mac, and the other one could enroll in pre-law at Drake. Why did people have to make such hard decisions, such *impossible* decisions? She scowled until the radio announcer intruded into her thoughts.

"An unexpected snowstorm is sweeping across the Mississippi valley and is now covering the eastern half of Iowa. A traveler's advisory is in effect for the next twenty-four hours. I-80 is closed east of Newton. I-35 is still open north of Des Moines, but it is becoming snow-packed and dangerous. Iowa motorists are advised to postpone all but emergency travel."

Nobody said anything for a few moments; then Jill spoke up. "We only have a few miles to go on I-80, don't we, Mom? And Newton is twenty or thirty miles east of here. We'll be okay."

"The snow seems to be building up pretty fast." Mac wiped steam from the window with his jacket sleeve and peered intently into the darkness.

"Good old Mac can dig us out if we get

stuck," Tom said. "He's a fast study with a shovel."

"Archaeologists seldom dig in snow, good buddy."

"Maybe we should stop at a motel, Mom," Jill said.

"But I have to get back," Tracy said. "Since I had this afternoon off, I'm supposed to do the late-evening check at the animal shelter tonight. If we don't get back . . ."

"If we don't get back, someone else can do it for you," Jill said. "Be practical. You act as if those stray dogs and cats actually belong to *you*, Tracy."

"I do feel responsible for them. And really sorry for them, too." She sighed; then her voice brightened. "But we did find homes for five dogs and two cats this week."

"I suppose *you* took four of them." Jill laughed. "You're such a soft touch, I can hardly believe it."

At first Jill's words irritated her, but on second thought she guessed Jill was right. She was a soft touch. Maybe that's why she wanted to be a lawyer, so she could help people in trouble.

"I don't think she's such a soft touch," Mac said, breaking into her thoughts. "I've been trying to get her to let me adopt a dog for two years now and she won't do it."

"We don't let people adopt pets unless they offer the pet a secure home situation." Tracy laughed. "Being mascot for a fraternity house

7

just doesn't qualify. Who's going to take care of the dog during vacations?"

"Spare me," Mac said. "I've heard it all before."

Again they drove in silence for a few moments, and Tracy listened to the thumpsquish of the windshield wipers and the sound of the tires zinging against the wet pavement. The music contest had ended at fourthirty, but it had been five before Jill had received her rating. Tracy glanced at her watch. 5:20. And it was already dark.

"Mother, how can you see?" Jill leaned forward, peering through the windshield. "This is awful."

"We're almost at the entrance to the diagonal," Mrs. Sterling said. She slowed and let a silver semitruck go ahead of her onto the narrow, hilly highway that led to Marshalltown. "I don't usually like to follow a semi, but I think I'll let this one lead us home."

Tracy relaxed a bit as Mrs. Sterling followed at a safe distance behind the truck, using the red glow from its taillights to show her where the highway was. She felt as if they were inside one of those snow scene paperweights which somebody had suddenly turned upside down. But that fanciful thinking ended abruptly as the truck slowed. When Mrs. Sterling braked their car, it almost skidded onto the shoulder.

"Mom," Jill said. "This storm is building faster than that news announcer said it was. I think we should stop at a motel. Really.

Just because Tracy thinks she has to get back is no reason for us to take chances."

Mrs. Sterling drove along without replying until Jill repeated her message.

"Jill, think," her mother said. "We're on the diagonal. There aren't any motels along here. We're doing fine. I'll just follow the truck home."

"Mrs. Sterling?" Mac leaned forward. "Maybe we should drop back just a little. We're coming to a lot of hills, and if that truck stalls on one of them, we'll stall, too."

"Just what we need — a backseat driver." Tom sighed.

"Just what we need — a motor mouth!" Mac retorted.

"You're right, Mac," Mrs. Sterling said. "There's no way we could get around a stalled truck, and there are several cars following us, I think. At least there were a few minutes ago. Right now I can't see any headlights."

Again they drove along with nobody speaking. Even Tom kept his mouth shut, a feat Tracy considered a near miracle. The wind, which had hit them head-on on the interstate, was now hitting them at an angle, and Tracy felt the car waver, gain momentum, then waver again. They followed the truck, creeping up a steep hill, and made it. The truck gained speed on the downgrade, but Mrs. Sterling kept a good distance behind it as it began its ascent of the next hill.

"This is one of the worst ones," Tom piped up. "The Crabtree Lake hill."

"How can *you* tell exactly where we are?" Mac demanded.

"Because I recognize that relay tower on our left. See that blinking red light? My dad and I come out here pheasant hunting sometimes. Once we get over this hill we'll have it made, Mrs. Sterling."

"*If* we get over it." Jill held her breath.

"Such optimism," Mac said, but now he released Tracy's hand and leaned forward as the car barely inched along.

"Come on, truck!" Tom begged. "Come on, fellow. You can do it."

"He's not going to make it." Mac groaned. "I can tell. And if we stop, we'll never get started again."

"But I can't pass him," Mrs. Sterling said. "The tires spin when I step on the gas, and, besides, I can't pass on a hill."

"There's a gravel road on our right," Tom said. "Can you see it? I know it's there somewhere. Maybe we could take it, drive around a square mile, and then get back on the diagonal ahead of the truck."

"No way," Jill said.

Tracy kept her own negative opinion to herself. That was Tom, always ready to leap.

"I'm going to try for it," Mrs. Sterling said. "It's our only chance to keep going."

"I suppose it's no worse to be stuck on gravel than to be stuck on the highway." Jill sighed as her mother peered through the windshield and then turned to the right.

For a moment Tracy thought they had missed the road, but then the car steadied itself and they headed on into the blinding blizzard with the wind tearing at the car as if trying to overturn it.

"Watch the speedometer," Mac said.

"By all means," Tom said. "Wouldn't want to be caught speeding."

"I'm watching the *mileage*, bright boy," Mac replied. "When we've gone almost a mile we can start looking for the intersection where we'll turn left."

"Good thinking, Mac," Mrs. Sterling said. "We're going to make it home."

Tracy chewed on her lower lip as she watched the odometer for another half mile or so. Then suddenly the car jolted, fishtailed into a skid, and stopped.

"What'd we hit?" Tom rolled down his window and tried to peer out.

"Close that, you idiot," Mac shouted.

Tracy brushed snow from her face, feeling its wet coldness against her cheeks and her fingers. She knew without being told that they had hit a snowdrift. She heard the tires spin and felt the vibration of the floorboard as Mrs. Sterling raced the motor, urging the car forward. Then she shifted into reverse and raced the motor again. The tires screamed a protest.

They were stuck.

· 2 ·

Jill peered out into the blinding snowstorm. "Now what are we going to do?"

"Wait it out, I suppose," her mother said. "What else can we do?"

"How much gas have we got?" Mac asked.

"A little over a quarter of a tank," Mrs. Sterling said.

"That won't last long." Mac sighed. "Better turn off the engine until we really get cold. Then we can turn it on long enough to get the heater working."

"Got any blankets?" Tom asked. "My dad always carries blankets and a sleeping bag in his car trunk."

"Good for him," Mac said. "We weren't expecting a blizzard."

"You're always supposed to expect a blizzard in Iowa in the winter," Tom countered.

"Cork it, you two," Tracy said. "Maybe a

couple of us could walk somewhere for help. I'm wearing boots and my heavy coat."

"I won't have any of you trying to walk anywhere," Mrs. Sterling said. "You'd freeze to death."

"It's always better to stay with the car," Tom agreed. "This is a real experience, you know. I may be able to write a blizzard article when we get back."

"If we get back," Jill said.

Tracy felt Mac pull her to him and felt his warm breath on her ear as he whispered, "I vote you the girl I'd most like to be stranded with in a blizzard."

She snuggled closer to him, glad for his warmth, his nearness. This is the way it could be for the rest of my life, she thought. Mac always near. Then once more Tom nudged her with his elbow.

"Hey! I know where we are and I've got an idea."

"I know where we are, too, Tom," Jill said. "We're out in the middle of nowhere."

"No, we aren't," Tom said. "I mean, we are, of course, but I think we're near the old Graydon house."

Tracy turned toward Tom. "Really?" She had driven by Graydon Place many times with her father because his law firm was in charge of the Graydon estate. He drove by the property now and then to check on the condition of the old, abandoned house.

"I'm sure," Tom said. "I tell you I come out this way with Dad a lot. We've driven about a half mile on this road, and the Graydon place should be right over there to our left. If we could battle that wind and wade through the drifts, we might be able to get inside and build a fire or something."

"But . . . Graydon Place is supposed to be *haunted*," Jill said. "People say they've seen strange lights at night and heard crying and . . . and I'm going to stay right here in the car."

"I think we should stay put," Mrs. Sterling said. "Not that I believe for a minute that the house is haunted, but if we became separated or something I'd feel so responsible."

"I'm not going to any haunted house," Mac said.

"Oh, come on, Mac." Tracy turned to look at him. "The place isn't really haunted."

"How do you know?"

"Dad's handling the Graydon estate. The old house is just an old house, that's all. Dad says the property has been in the Graydon family for over a hundred years. He hires a man to farm the few acres of land, but nobody has lived in the house since Mary Graydon died over twenty years ago."

"Maybe nobody has lived there *because* it's haunted," Jill said.

"No, it's because there are no Graydons left but six elderly, distant cousins who live in California and who don't want to be bothered with a small farm and an old house in Iowa."

"Why don't they sell it then?" Jill asked.

"There's a stigma about the place," Tracy said. "Of course it isn't haunted, but there are stories about strange, unexplained deaths, stuff like that."

"I can understand why the place hasn't been sold," Mrs. Sterling said. "People shy away from a house with a history of tragedy."

"Wish I was in California right now," Tom said. "Those Graydon cousins aren't so dumb. Sunshine. Palm trees. Sand beach."

"Dream on," Mac said.

Tracy listened to the wind roar around the car, watched the snow swirl, felt the penetrating cold numb her feet, her fingers, her nose. Could they last out the night? She snuggled closer to Mac. Mrs. Sterling turned the engine on intermittently, warming them for a few moments, but once she turned the heater off, the car soon grew cold.

"I think we should try to walk to the Graydon place," Tracy said at last. "How about running the engine and the heater until we're really warm, and then we'll get out and try to find the house?"

"We're almost out of gas," Mac pointed out. "No gas, no heat."

"Dad says the house is still furnished," Tracy said. "I've never seen the inside, but Dad says it's just like it was the day old Mary Graydon died. Surely there's a stove and something we could use to make a fire. It's only eight o'clock. We can't last in this cold until morning."

Mac snapped on his transistor radio. For a few minutes they listened to a furnace commercial; then the announcer spoke.

"Again, a repeat of the traveler's advisory. Winds are gusting to fifty miles an hour and all highways in the area are now closed. The storm has worsened, and it is expected to continue at least until midmorning. It's a good night to stay home by the fireside. Keep tuned to KFJB for an hourly update on weather conditions."

"A good night to stay by your fireside. Bah!" Tom exclaimed.

Mrs. Sterling started the car, turned on the heater, and in a few moments Tracy felt herself warming up.

"I think we should try to make it to the Graydon place," she said again, hoping they would listen to her this time. "Let's all get out, join hands, and walk to our left until we reach the fence."

"What fence?" Jill asked.

"All the cornfields around here are fenced," Tracy said. "You know that. Once we find the fence, we can follow it until we reach the yard where the house stands."

"Sounds reasonable," Mac said. "I vote that we try it."

"Me, too," Tom said.

"Maybe we should," Mrs. Sterling agreed reluctantly. "I have a flashlight in the glove compartment, and we can leave the car lights on. If we don't find the house, we'd surely be able to see the lights and find our way back to the car."

"But if we do find the house, then the car battery will run down," Jill said. "Nobody will want to come back and turn off the lights."

"We're not going to get out of here without being towed, anyway," Tracy said, wishing she could give Jill a shake. "What's a dead battery matter if it saves our lives?"

"Saves our lives?"

"Yeah," Mac said through chattering teeth. "People have been known to freeze to death, you know. We're not just playing games out here."

"Let's go then," Mrs. Sterling said. "Everyone put on everything you have with you. Hats. Gloves. Scarves. And button up your coats."

"I'll lead the way," Tom said. "I think I know about where the house should be."

Nobody argued with him, and Mrs. Sterling gave him the flashlight after they got out of the car. Tracy's eyes watered and she felt the wind blow up under her skirt, chilling her knees and thighs until she couldn't even feel them. Usually she wore slacks or jeans. And so did Jill. But today they had dressed up for the music contest.

Mac took Tom's hand, she took Mac's hand, and Jill took her other hand.

"Wait," Mrs. Sterling shouted. "I stopped at the grocery this morning. I've got a little food." She reached for a small, brown sack; then she clutched at Jill's arm as they all lowered their heads into the gale and plodded across the road.

Tracy ducked her head as the wind and snow seemed to swirl from all directions. She tucked her chin into the collar of her coat and struggled through drifts, feeling the heavy, wet snow seep over her boot tops and slip down inside.

"Here it is!" Tom shouted.

"The house?" Mac asked.

"No, you turkey. The fence!"

Tracy had never been so scared in all her life. The frigid night was like a giant magnet pulling all the energy from her body, sapping her strength. She had read stories about people being stranded in blizzards, freezing to death, but she thought it happened to other people. Not to her. They walked close enough to the fence to scrape against it with their feet as they pushed forward, and after a while they reached the end of it. Tracy sensed that Mac was pulling her along. If it weren't for Mac she couldn't go any farther.

Tom turned at an angle, fighting against swirling wind and snow. "The house should be this way," he shouted over his shoulder.

Tracy thought she could walk no farther. Snow had matted in her eyelashes, her hands and feet were numb, and freezing air seared her nose and throat until she could hardly breathe. But she hated to be the one to give up since she had suggested this idea. Why hadn't they stayed in the car? When Tom fell, they all went down like a line-up of dominoes.

She knew she couldn't struggle back to her feet. Her face was buried in the snow and at first she couldn't focus on Tom's words.

"The porch!" Tom shouted as he rose and floundered ahead. "I stumbled on the porch steps!"

"We made it." Mac spoke softly, leaning over Tracy, trying to help her up. His tone told her that he hadn't really believed they would make it. Her heart was pounding so fast she couldn't reply, but she found the strength to stand, to take a few more steps.

Now they all crowded onto the porch, the boys shouting, stamping their feet, and shouting some more.

"What are we waiting for?" Tom asked, slapping everyone on the back. "Let's go inside." He hurried to the door and turned the knob.

The door was locked.

· 3 ·

Tracy stood with her back to the whirling snow, trying to scrunch her neck and head down into the upturned collar of her coat as she shouted above the roar of the wind. "Oh, I forgot — the key's in Dad's safe."

"We'll have to break in." Mac eased Tom aside and tried the doorknob again.

"Oh!" Tom pointed at a window and stood closer to Jill. "I saw a light. I did! Through the window. Just for an instant."

"Impossible," Mrs. Sterling said. "Don't be silly."

"But I did," Tom insisted. "I know I did."

"Probably just the reflection of car lights flashing against the windowpane," Mac shouted. "The scientific mind scoffs at ghosts."

"Sure," Jill said, when the wind died down for a moment. "Of course your car-light theory is totally scientific, especially since traffic on the highway has stopped."

"Well . . ." Mac hesitated, his teeth chattering as he tried to think of an answer. "Forget the lights. Let's see about getting inside the house."

"Swamp gas," Tom said.

"Swamp gas?" Tracy huddled closer to Mac, wishing someone would hurry and break the door open, yet not wanting to be the one. It seemed so much like vandalism.

"Swamp gas," Tom repeated. "Whenever anyone sees unexplained lights, they're always explained away as rotting vegetation and swamp gas. Should be a lot of that around here on a night like this."

"Nobody else *saw* any lights." Mac ignored Tom's sarcasm. "It was your imagination. How about it, man? Think we can put our shoulders to that door?" Mac stepped back and then lunged forward, thrusting his weight against the gray, weathered oak. The door groaned but held firm.

"Wait." Tracy grabbed Mac's arm before he could make another try. "If you hit the door too hard it may pop off the hinges. That'd let a lot of cold inside. We could break one of those small windows, unlock it, and raise it. That way we'd only have a small hole to patch up later."

"Good idea." Mac backed away from the door. "What'll we break the window with?"

Tracy yanked off her scarf. "I'll hold this

over the glass to keep flying shards from cutting us; then, Mac, how about using your shoe? The heel?"

"I'll try."

Mrs. Sterling aimed her flashlight across the porch, shining it on a window to the right of the door.

"A screen." Tom poked at the screen, breaking the rotten, rusted wire easily and ripping it from its gray frame. "There. Let's have the scarf, Tracy."

Tom held the scarf in place while Mac tapped the windowpane with the heel of his shoe. The gale howling under the eaves almost masked the sound of shattering glass.

"Careful!" Mrs. Sterling shouted. "Don't cut yourself."

Tom gave the scarf back to Tracy as Mac reached through the hole in the pane and fumbled at the lock. In moments the window was open.

"I'm not going in first," Jill announced.

"I am." Mac brushed draperies aside and lifted one leg over the sill.

"Here, take the flashlight." Mrs. Sterling handed him the light, and Mac eased on through the window and then turned to offer Tracy a hand. Once inside and still holding Mac's hand, Tracy peered into the frigid darkness, listening to the wind rattle the windows. The house gave off a musty smell of mice and stale air and some other odors Tracy couldn't identify. It reminded her of the Spook House at Adventureland. But at least they were out of the storm.

Mac helped Jill over the sill, then Mrs. Sterling, then Tom. When they were all inside, Tracy closed the window again and lifted the hem of the rotting drapery, stuffing it into the jagged hole as best she could. Mac directed the flashlight beam around the room, an old-fashioned parlor with a threadbare Brussels carpet. Tracy saw a maroon, velvet-cushioned sofa, a matching arm chair, and two black Windsor rockers. There was an old walnut library table, a walnut bookcase near the window, and a green flowerpot on a tall oak pedestal.

"A fireplace!" Jill stepped onto the red brick hearth. "We can make a fire and sit right beside it until help comes."

"Let's see what else we have here first before we settle down to be cozy around a fire." Mac led the way into a dining room, and Tracy saw a round oak table and six straight-backed chairs with wine and gray needlepoint cushions. It was as if they were waiting for someone to come to dinner. An inner chill made her shudder. She was being as silly as Tom and Jill. Nobody was about to come in.

An oak sideboard stood on one side of the room and a glass-front china closet stood on the other. Dishes. Tracy could see white plates bordered in gold, crystal goblets, and white cups and saucers.

Mac walked on into the kitchen and flashed the light over an old gas cookstove, a white-topped utility table, and three pine chairs. At the side of an old-fashioned white cupboard that almost touched the ceiling, a door opened into a large pantry.

"Maybe this was the milk room," Mrs. Sterling said. "I think these old houses used to have a special room for separating the cream from the milk."

"How about a fire in the fireplace now that we've had the grand tour?" Jill stamped her feet to warm them. "This place is as cold as the car was."

"Here are steps leading into a cellar." Mac flashed the light down into a steep, stone stairwell where gray cobwebs hung, swaying in an eerie draft.

Tracy cringed and held onto Mac's arm. "We don't need to go down there. No way."

Mac led them back to the entryway. "Here's a stairway leading to the second floor."

"Let's take a look up there," Mrs. Sterling said. "Maybe there are beds."

"Mom! We're not going to sleep here, are we? All we need is a fire. Please, a fire!"

Tracy was beginning to share Jill's apprehensive feelings about the old house, yet she knew they would have to sleep somewhere.

"I suppose you can sit up all night if you want to," Mrs. Sterling said, "but let's go see what's upstairs, okay?"

Mac took Tracy's hand as Mrs. Sterling led the way up the creaking stairs, and Tracy noticed that the stale smell grew worse the higher they went.

"Hope those flashlight batteries hold up," Tom said.

"You could have gone forever without saying that," Tracy groaned.

"They seem strong enough," Mrs. Sterling said. "They're fairly new."

For a moment they stood huddled at the top of the stairwell as Mac flashed the light over green floral-print wallpaper.

"Looks like three bedrooms up here," Tracy said. "And a lot of closets."

"Let's check out the bedrooms," Mrs. Sterling said.

They followed her to the doorway of a room with a walnut four-poster bed and matching dresser. Mrs. Sterling approached the bed, and Tracy saw her shudder slightly as she touched the yellow-and-orange quilt.

"It looks just as it must have looked when the Graydons lived here. Sheets. Blankets. Quilt."

The room smelled dank and musty, but Tracy didn't comment. They trooped to the next room where there was a brass bed and a brown painted dresser and chest. An old iron bedstead and a sturdy oak dresser and chair stood in the third bedroom.

"Let's go back downstairs and build a fire," Jill said. "Please!"

"Where do these other doors lead?" Tom began opening closet doors and closing them again. The third door he opened caused them all to gasp. "This one leads to a third floor," Tom said. "An attic."

"I'm not going up there," Jill said. "No way."

"Why don't we build a fire in the fireplace?" Tracy asked, thinking they had seen enough of the old house. She didn't believe in ghosts, but she could sympathize with Tom and Jill. The place was cold and dank and *eerie*. There was no other word for it. "Let's go down and see what we can find that will burn."

"Wait," Mrs. Sterling said. "Mac, see if you can get another weather bulletin on your radio."

"As if there's anything else on!" Tom exclaimed. "The weather is big news tonight."

The radio crackled and hummed, and they listened to recorded music for a few minutes before the announcer began speaking. There was so much static they could hardly understand his words.

". . . no letup in the blizzard . . . conditions worsening as a whiteout . . . stay off the highways . . . maintenance crews unable to work . . ." Static crackled and popped, drowning out the rest of the bulletin.

"We're stuck here for the night, that's for sure," Tracy said, trying to keep her voice light and bright. "Come on, we've got to get a fire going."

"Wait," Mrs. Sterling said again. "I know we all would like to see a fire in that fireplace, but I'm not sure that building a fire is the wisest thing to do."

"Why not, Mom?"

"I looked around downstairs. There's only a small stack of firewood. Just a few pieces. If we keep a fire going we may have to burn furniture, and, after all, the place isn't ours. We're trespassing."

"We're also freezing," Jill said.

"What time is it?" Tom asked.

Tracy looked at the luminous dial on her watch. "Almost nine-thirty." She thought of her parents. And who had taken her place at the animal shelter?

"It's a long time until morning," Mrs. Sterling said. "I think we should go to bed to try to keep warm and not think about building a fire in the fireplace until morning."

"Go to bed in this creepy place!" Jill half whispered the words. "Sleep in those musty, old beds. They're probably full of moths and . . . and yuck!"

"Granted, it's not the Holiday Inn," Mac said. "But I think your mother's right, Jill. We've done a lot of kidding, but this is a serious situation. We don't know how long we're going to be stranded here, and it's just sound thinking to conserve that little supply of wood downstairs."

Tracy sided with Mac. "We can poke around in the closets and find more blankets and we can even toss some of these braided throw rugs onto the beds for more warmth."

"I'm with Mac and Tracy," Tom said. "Those beds are the warmest places we're going to find tonight. Mac and I'll bunk in the brass bed, okay?"

"Mom, you and I can share the four-poster, I suppose," Jill said, "but that leaves Tracy alone."

Tom laughed. "Five of us crowded into three rooms is hardly an 'alone' situation for anyone."

"I don't mind," Tracy said. "All I want to do is to get warm." White lies. She did mind. This old house was creepy and she wished she were home.

While Mac held the light, Mrs. Sterling went through the closets, pulling out every available blanket and dividing them equally among the three beds. An extra army blanket went to Tracy because she was sleeping alone.

"I saw some candles downstairs," Mrs. Sterling said. "Tall red ones. They were in the kitchen on that white cupboard by the pantry."

"Why haven't we been using them and saving the flashlight battery?" Jill asked.

"There's always danger of fire when you use candles," her mother said, "but of course we'll use them if we really need to. What I was thinking is that perhaps we each should have a candle at bedside in case of some sort of emergency."

"Yeah," Mac agreed. "We can't split a flashlight three ways. I'll go down and find the candles."

"And leave us here in the dark?" Jill asked.

"Come along if you want to," Mac invited.

Jill sighed. "I'll stay here."

Tracy felt Jill reach for her hand. The dark was like black cotton blocking off all vision, and they could hear strange creaks and groans coming from different parts of the house. Now and then something popped like a small firecracker.

"What was *that?*" Jill's grip tightened on Tracy's hand.

"Just these old timbers contracting from the cold," Mrs. Sterling said. "All houses do that."

Tracy thought about Mrs. Sterling's words. She couldn't remember any creaks and groans in her home in town. When Mac returned with the candles he distributed them one per room.

"I even found some old jar lids to use as candleholders," he said.

"I have some book matches." Mrs. Sterling reached into her purse, brought out matches, and they lighted the candles, melting a bit of the red wax into the jar lids, then setting the candles in them to hold them upright. The wavering candlelight was almost worse than the dark, Tracy thought, as she watched the weird shadows the flames cast on the walls and the ceiling.

"Sweet dreams," Tom called to the others as he and Mac went into their room.

"If anyone has a problem, call me," Mrs.

Sterling said. "Don't hesitate to wake me up."

"Who's really planning to sleep?" Jill asked. "I know I'll stare at the ceiling all night long. This place reminds me of the midnight horror movies on TV."

Tracy agreed with Jill, but she kept quiet. She didn't care if she slept or not; she just wanted to get warm. She thought longingly of her cozy bed at home as she looked around the strange, cold room. Blue walls. Blue curtains. Bare pine floors, except for the throw rugs. The mattress on the iron bed seemed comfortable enough. Maybe she would sleep, if she ever got warm. Hadn't she read something about freezing to death if you went to sleep in the cold? But with all these covers it surely wouldn't be that cold.

She lifted a multicolored throw rug from the floor and laid it on the foot of the bed, handling it gently so the dust wouldn't fly. Should she wear her boots to bed? She almost giggled at the thought, yet the idea of removing them in the icy room made her cringe. She decided to keep them on. She turned the bedcovers back, wondering who had slept in the bed last. Mary Graydon? It was not a thought she cared to dwell on. This bed had no sheets, just blankets over the blue-and-white striped mattress ticking.

Before she snuffed the candle Tracy studied the room carefully, noting the position of the door into the hallway and where the closet door was. Then her gaze fell on a gold-framed portrait hanging on the east wall. Some long-gone Graydon, she thought. She picked up the candle and stepped nearer to the picture, examining it carefully.

The girl in the painting seemed to be about her own age. She was plump and she wore her blond hair in a braid-and-crown effect that called attention to her piercing blue eyes, the stubborn tilt of her chin, and her full lips that looked as if they pouted more than they smiled. The girl wore an ankle-length gown of peacock blue satin with a draped skirt and tight-fitting bodice. Her short cloth boots with patent toecaps showed beneath the hem of her gown. But what held Tracy's attention was the girl's complexion. Her skin was the color of old bones.

"I wonder who she was," Tracy murmured aloud. She looked at the picture for another moment; then she walked back to the bed, crawled under the blankets, and snuffed the candle.

For a while she lay awake, but gradually she grew sleepy, drew herself into a ball, and closed her eyes. She wasn't sure when she dozed off, but she awakened with a start when she heard Jill sobbing. She sat up, pulling the blankets to her chin.

"Jill?" She half whispered the word. "Jill, where are you? What's wrong?"

The sobbing stopped.

Tracy saw a glow of light coming from the vicinity of the portrait.

She blinked and rubbed her eyes. Was she

imagining things? No. It wasn't her imagination. A young teenage girl stood in the room staring at the portrait.

A chill feathered along Tracy's nape, yet she had no sense of being in great danger from the intruder. She wanted to call Mac, yet she held back.

"Who . . . who are you?" Tracy asked quietly, trying to forget Tom's words about the house being haunted. This girl certainly seemed real enough. "Who *are* you?" She repeated her question.

The girl turned, and her face and clothing gave off an ethereal glow.

Tracy felt herself shaking. She couldn't breathe.

The room was pitch black. How was she able to see this girl? Her mouth and throat grew so dry she couldn't repeat her question, nor could she call for Mac or Mrs. Sterling. But now the girl answered.

"I'm Victoria Graydon." Her voice was soft as the flutter of dove wings.

Somehow Tracy breathed again and found the presence of mind to light the candle at her bedside. The girl who called herself Victoria Graydon was of slight build and she wore a lilac-colored cotton dress accented with a frothy lace collar and cuffs. The skirt of her pale dress fell gracefully to her ankles. She had blond, waist-length hair, and, although her eyes were the same blue as the eyes of the girl in the painting, Victoria's gaze didn't penetrate. Her eyes seemed dreamy and sad and her full lips were quivering.

"What are you doing here?" Tracy found she could speak. But she didn't call out.

"What are *you* doing here?" Victoria Graydon asked.

"Five of us were caught in the blizzard. We broke into the house to keep from freezing in the car. Do you — I mean — do you *live* here?"

"I used to live here. Long ago." The girl began to sob softly again.

"What's the matter?" Tracy's voice shook. She knew she was talking to a ghost, yet this girl seemed more frightened than she did. "Why are you crying?"

"I'm crying because I murdered Rowena." Victoria nodded toward the painting. "My sister, Rowena."

"But, but . . ." Tracy could think of no sensible thing to say and she was shaking so badly she knew she couldn't stand, couldn't leave the room no matter how much she wanted to.

"I killed her long ago," Victoria said. "But Rowena's death is still on my conscience. I can't rest. I can't rest. I need help."

"Why did you murder your sister?" Tracy whispered the words. If this girl had killed once, would she kill again?

"It was a personal matter," Victoria said. "A family matter. I am so sorry I did it. So terribly sorry."

Tracy thought for a moment. She was the

one who needed help, not Victoria. Yet she didn't want to scream for help. Somehow it didn't seem to be a screaming situation. Something about Victoria Graydon made her want to help the girl. *Soft touch.* Jill's words replayed in her mind. How could she help a girl who had murdered her sister . . . a long time ago?

Tracy got out of bed. She had to have help. She couldn't handle the situation alone any longer. Her first impulse was to call Mac. Then she decided not to. He was so big. And she knew he would be on the offensive. He might scare this girl, and somehow Tracy felt very sorry for her.

"Where are you going?" Victoria asked, as Tracy headed for the doorway.

"I'll be right back." She hurried to the room where Mrs. Sterling and Jill were sleeping in the four-poster.

"What are you doing up, Tracy?" Jill asked the minute Tracy cleared her throat and stepped into the bedroom. "I thought I heard you talking to the boys."

"I wasn't talking to the boys, Jill. Get up. Come with me. There's a girl in my room who says she's Victoria Graydon."

"You've been dreaming," Jill said.

"I think she's a ghost," Tracy whispered.

"Then I'm not going near your room. Come in here and close the door."

"Please come with me, Jill."

"What's going on, girls?" Mrs. Sterling sat up, blinking sleepily.

"Tracy says there's someone in her room," Jill said.

Mrs. Sterling bolted upright. "If those boys are playing tricks I'll . . ."

"It wasn't the boys, Mrs. Sterling. It was a girl. Victoria Graydon."

"You've been having a nightmare, Tracy." Mrs. Sterling got out of bed and stood next to her. "Come on, I'll show you there's nobody in your room; then you can spend the rest of the night in here with us. We can make room for three in the bed. We shouldn't have left you alone after all the talk about ghosts."

"Mrs. Sterling, there really *is* a girl in my room." Tracy led the way back to her bedroom.

When the three of them entered there was nobody else there.

Only Rowena Graydon stared at them with her hard, arrogant gaze.

35

• 4 •

Tracy scowled and looked all around the room, peering into the closet as if someone might be hiding there, yet there were only three of them in the room. She felt so foolish. Had she been dreaming?

Mrs. Sterling patted her on the shoulder as they huddled in the cold. "You just had a nightmare, Tracy. And no wonder. This creaking old house, the cold. Why don't you come sleep with Jill and me for the rest of the night? We'll just close the door on this room."

"I don't want to crowd you and Jill." Tracy knew she wasn't going to sleep a wink the rest of the night.

"Then I'll sleep in here with you," Mrs. Sterling said.

"And leave me all alone?" Jill's voice shrilled with indignation and fear.

36

"What's going on?" Mac called from down the hall.

"Nothing, Mac," Tracy replied. "Everything's fine."

"Tracy just had a nightmare," Mrs. Sterling called to Mac.

Tracy breathed a sigh of relief. She didn't want Mac and Tom laughing at her.

"Jill," Mrs. Sterling said, "I'm not allowing Tracy to stay in this room alone. I know how a nightmare can upset a person. If you don't want to be alone, then you sleep in here with Tracy. I don't mind being alone."

Jill peered around the room, then shrugged. "Well, okay, I guess. Could we leave the candle lit?"

"I suppose so," her mother said. "It'll probably burn out after a while, but we won't be needing it." She set the candle on the dresser, placing it on a piece of old newspaper so the melted paraffin wouldn't damage anything.

"I'm sorry I wakened you, Mrs. Sterling," Tracy said, glad that Jill was going to spend the rest of the night with her, glad Mrs. Sterling had supplied her with an excuse for her behavior. A nightmare. Anyone could have a nightmare.

"I wish it were morning," Jill said.

"You girls call me if you need to." Mrs. Sterling's teeth chattered from the cold and she hurried back to her bedroom.

"Did you really see someone in here?" Jill

whispered, when her mother had gone and she and Tracy had crawled under the covers.

"I thought I did. There was this young girl dressed in old-fashioned clothes."

"It was just a dream," Jill said. "Really. It had to be. I know this house is supposed to be haunted, but I don't even like to think about it. Don't you really believe you just had a nightmare?"

Tracy didn't want to frighten Jill. She really wasn't sure what had happened. "I suppose it was just a dream, Jill. Let's forget it, okay?"

"Fine by me."

Tracy lay awake for a long time, watching the candle flame flicker in the draft that seeped around the window frames, listening to Jill's even breathing. Were her parents sleeping? She knew they were probably sitting up and worrying. She felt bad, yet she knew there was no way to call them.

The next morning Tracy got up quickly and ran a comb through her long hair. Peering into the mirror on the dresser she saw that she had patriotic eyes. Red, white, and blue. They burned from cold and lack of sleep, but she refrained from rubbing them and making them more bloodshot than they already were.

Nobody had to bother to dress because they all had slept in their clothes. Tracy would have laughed at their rumpled appearance if she hadn't been so cold. Jill had pulled her long hair into a ponytail, but her red blazer and plaid skirt looked as if someone had used them for dustcloths. And Tracy's own navy blazer and skirt looked even worse. Mac's gray flannel slacks were creased horizontally as well as vertically. Only Tom showed little effect of the night, but then Tom always looked sort of rumpled. She suspected that Tom tried to live up to what he considered a reporter's image — casual, at the ready under any circumstances.

Mac ran downstairs first, his footsteps shaking the house like thunder, and Tom followed him. By the time Tracy and Jill and Mrs. Sterling had straightened the beds, the boys had a fire blazing on the hearth.

"Ah, my favorite thing." Jill stretched her outspread fingers toward the fire. "Forget about brown paper packages tied up with string like the song says. Give me a hearth fire every time."

Tracy stood close to the blaze, too, trying to soak in its warmth. It was the first time she had realized that a fire could be so sensuous. She smelled the faint aroma of smoke, heard the burning wood crackle and pop, saw the blue-orange-gold of the flames. Taste? That was the only detail that was missing, or was it missing? The smell of the burning wood left a smoky taste on the back of her tongue.

"We've got news," Mac said. "There's a privy out back. We made a quick trip. It's still snowing, and there are deep drifts, but you'll survive out there."

"Thanks a lot," Jill said. "I thought maybe..."

"You expected hot and cold running maids, I presume," Tom teased.

"I'm starved," Mac said. "Really starved."

"What was all that chatter in the middle of the night?" Tom asked, looking at the girls.

"Tracy saw a ghost." Jill laughed. "It was hardly fair for *her* to see it when you and I were the ones who thought the house was haunted."

"A ghost?" Tom asked. "Hey, maybe there's another story here. Give, Tracy. Exactly what did you see?"

"There was this girl named Victoria Graydon." Tracy scowled at Jill, wishing she had kept quiet.

"Hey, she told you her name? Let me get my notepad."

"And I'll bet her form glowed with an ethereal light." Mac guffawed.

"And did she wear a costume from another century?" Tom slapped Tracy on the back.

Tracy walked to a window, pretending great interest in the storm. Suddenly she hated Tom's habit of backslapping. Someday he was going to slap the wrong person and that person would turn around and deck him. Yet it wasn't just Tom who irritated her. Most of all she felt hurt because Mac had laughed.

"Tracy just had a nightmare," Mrs. Sterling said. "Let's forget it and see what we can do to get ourselves out of here. I'm sure all your parents must be crazy with worry. I know I would be."

Mac joined Tracy at the window, slipping his arm around her waist. "I don't think we're going home soon, gang," he said. "It's still snowing. Take a look. I can't even see the car. It must be completely buried."

Reluctantly the others left the fireside to peer out the windows. Tracy softened toward Mac and forgave him for laughing, as she welcomed his embrace. She peered outside and saw drifts that banked halfway up the windows. In the front yard the howling wind had blown the snow into ten-foot drifts in some places; yet in other spots the ground was almost bare.

"The whole world looks like a white desert," Tracy said. "Dunes of snow, if there could be such a thing."

Mac had flicked on his transistor the minute he got up, and as the announcer's voice spluttered into the room everyone gathered around to listen.

"There has been no letup in the blizzard conditions," the announcer said. "Stay in your homes. If an emergency arises, dial 911. The mayor and the police are working to organize a snowmobile rescue squad. Anyone with a snowmobile who wants to help out will be welcome. Report to the municipal building. Keep tuned to this station for the latest news on local, national, and international fronts."

"No letup." Tracy groaned. "What are we going to do?"

"Better get good and warm." Tom ran his fingers through his hair until it stood in dark tufts. "When this fire dies out, well, there isn't much more wood."

"How about food?" Mac asked. "Mrs. Sterling, didn't you say something about groceries?"

"I've got a couple of cans of pork and beans, a wedge of cheese, and some canned peaches. Stuff probably froze in here last night."

"So we'll thaw it out," Mac said. "Better do it before the fire goes out."

"Let's think about this a minute," Tracy said. "We really haven't looked around here in the daylight."

"You're not expecting to find food, are you?" Jill asked. "Not in a house that's been vacant for twenty years."

"No, but we might find something to burn. We could look in the cellar and see if there's anything down there that wouldn't be missed."

"But in case there isn't," Tom said, "let's get those beans over the fire before it goes out. Hot beans will be better than cold beans. And we can melt snow into water. Don't have to worry about not having enough to drink."

"Come on, girls," Mac said. "Let Tom play cook while we scout around in that cellar. I've got the flashlight."

42

Mac went first, and Tracy and Jill followed him down rough stone stairs into the black hole of a basement. Tracy flinched as she felt a cobweb brush her cheek, and the smell of mice was so strong she breathed through her mouth to avoid it. Mac flashed the light on the steps until they reached the dirt floor; then he arced the beam over the walls, over gray web-laced rafters. Tracy heard a scrambling sound in a corner to her left and felt a sudden draft as someone upstairs opened a door.

"What was that?" Jill clutched Tracy's arm and backed toward the steps as something squeaked in a far corner.

"Just mice," Mac said. "They're more afraid of you than you are of them."

"Want to bet?" Jill hung back.

"Hey, there's an old fruit cellar or something." Mac opened a splintered pine door and flashed the light into a cubbyhole of a room which was lined with shelves on three sides. Tracy thought she could smell onions. She sniffed again. Would onion odor cling for two decades?

Tracy gasped as an idea hit her. "Hey! Wood! The shelves. We can pull them out and burn them!"

"Great!" Mac said. "Let's go tell the others." He grabbed Tracy's hand and pulled her toward the steps.

Tracy was glad to go upstairs. The cellar had seemed warmer than the upper parts of the house, but she hated the smell, the webs, the sound of scampering mice. She shuddered. When Mac reached the top of the steps and blurted the news of the wooden shelves, Tom and Mrs. Sterling smiled as if it were the best news they had ever heard.

"I guess we're going to survive," Mrs. Sterling said. "Surely the snowplows will be able to get through the drifts by afternoon. They'll have the highways cleared."

"Sure," Jill agreed. "But we're not on the highway, remember? We're on the gravel road. State maintenance crews will go into action quicker than the county crews."

For the first time in her life Tracy knew what it was to be really hungry. She hadn't eaten since noon the day before. "We'd better ration the food, gang. It might have to last us all day."

"You really know how to hurt a guy," Mac said, grinning at her.

Tom pulled up one of the Windsor rockers and began to write in his notebook.

"What are you doing?" Mac asked.

"Taking notes on all this, buddy. A writer has to be accurate. I'm writing down exactly how it is here, exactly how I feel."

"Well, I feel hungry," Mac said. "Put that in your notes somewhere."

"We're not the first ones to take refuge here," Mrs. Sterling said. "I found some old newspapers in the kitchen. One of them is less than a month old. And there's a box of crackers that seems okay to me. I broke a piece off one of them and it didn't taste too stale."

"Who do you suppose?" Tracy asked, thinking she should remember to tell her father. "How could anyone get in?"

"Just like we did," Mac said. "Break in."

"But I didn't notice any other broken windows," Tracy said.

"Have you really looked?" Mac asked.

"No. No, I really haven't, I guess. But I will. Later." Tracy saw that Mrs. Sterling had removed a grate from the kitchen stove, placed it in the fireplace, and set the opened can of beans on it. She had set saucers and forks on the oak table in the dining room. Tracy's stomach growled. How were five of them going to survive on one small can of beans?

But they managed, each eating a small portion of the beans and drinking a lot of the melted snow. Tracy was surprised at how much snow it took to make even a small glass of water. Jill and Tracy kept working on the snow-to-water detail while Mac and Tom washed the saucers and forks.

"We'll have cheese and crackers for lunch," Mrs. Sterling said.

"You really think the crackers are okay?" Tracy asked.

"I'll eat them," Mac said.

"Not me," Jill said. "This will be my diet day."

After they had cleaned up their mess and had a supply of water handy, they sat on the floor around the fire listening to the radio. Tracy groaned as she heard the announcer read their names as missing persons.

"If only we could get word to someone that we're okay," Tracy said.

"But we can't," Mac pointed out. "Might as well forget it."

They listened to the radio until the news went off the air; then Tom and Mac went to the cellar and returned with shelving to build up the fire.

"Maybe someone will see smoke curling from the chimney and come investigate," Tracy said.

"It could happen, I suppose," Mac said. "But who will see? There aren't many houses nearby, and nobody can pass by on the road."

Tracy stood. "We can't just sit here all day. Let's investigate the third floor since we didn't go up there last night. We might find some more blankets or something."

"You're not planning to spend another night here, are you?" Jill asked.

Nobody spoke. Tracy knew that the thought of being stranded for another night loomed in the backs of all their minds. She could hear the wind howling and so far there was no letup in the snow. And even when the snow stopped, the wind would continue. At least it usually did. Even if crews managed to open roads, snowdrifts would build up very quickly.

"Let's just go upstairs and take a good look around." Tracy stood. "This house really is a showplace of sorts. All this antique furniture and stuff. I wish I knew more about it."

"I wish we were out of here," Mac said. "But I wouldn't mind taking a look at antiques. I think they're interesting."

When Tracy started up the stairs, Mac followed along and she was glad. She wasn't all that brave, and she couldn't forget Victoria Graydon. Ghost? Nightmare? She might never be sure.

On the second floor they looked in all the closets which they hadn't bothered to examine carefully the previous night. Most of them were empty. A few had old clothes and books stored in them. Tracy shivered. The fireplace warmed only a small part of the living room. It was still cold everywhere else.

"Hey, look at this balcony," Mac called from the bedroom he had shared with Tom. "There's a door here that opens onto the roof over a porch."

Tracy joined him, peering out at the snow-covered balcony. "Must be nice in the summertime. Come on, Mac. Let's explore the attic."

The stairway to the third floor was short but it was also narrow, and there was no handrail. Tracy went first, and when she reached the top of the stairwell she almost turned back, there were so many cobwebs hanging from the rafters.

"Just look at this place, Mac! It's like a ballroom. No furniture at all. I'll bet the Graydons used to have parties up here, dances maybe." With one eye on the cobwebs she walked around, looking out the dormer windows into the white outside. Mac followed her, also eyeing the cobwebs that dangled thick as Spanish moss in some places.

Suddenly Tracy stopped and sniffed. What a strange smell. It reminded her of her dad's pipe tobacco — pleasant, aromatic. Then in the next instant she didn't smell it at all.

"What's the matter?" Mac asked.

"I thought I smelled pipe smoke." Tracy laughed. "Must be something they're burning in the fireplace."

"Maybe your ghost smokes." Mac laughed.

"She was hardly the pipe type." Tracy tried to forget the smell and she was sorry she had mentioned it. Mac had laughed at her again. "Wonder where those two doors at the opposite end of this room lead?"

"Probably just to under-the-eaves storage space," Mac said. "I'm cold. Let's go back to the fire."

"Let's take a quick look first." Tracy walked to one of the doors at the far end of the room and tugged on the black iron latch which lifted easily enough. But the door was warped, and the bottom of it dragged on the floor.

"Help me, Mac."

"Why bother?" Mac asked, but he helped Tracy lift up on the door latch until they managed to scrape the door open.

"See?" Mac said. "I told you. Nothing there at all."

Tracy poked her head into a very small room that she guessed might at one time have been used for a sewing room or maybe just extra storage space. There was nothing in it now. Mac helped again and they closed the door.

"Let's take a look in the other one," Tracy said.

"I'm ready to go back downstairs." Mac sneezed. "I'm freezing, and we're really stirring up a lot of dust up here."

Tracy looked at the floor, at their footprints that had smeared the dust on the wide-planked pine. She sneezed, too. Mac was heading for the stairs, but Tracy was just starting toward the door at the other end of the room when they heard strange music.

"What on earth?" She ran to the stairs and started down and Mac followed her. When they reached the first floor they found Tom cranking the handle of an old-time phonograph, as a scratchy melody floated into the room.

"Al Jolson," Mrs. Sterling said. "A real golden oldie."

They listened to a stack of old-time records, listened to Mac's transistor, and tried to pretend they weren't hungry. Mrs. Sterling rationed out cheese and crackers at noon, peaches for supper, and somehow the day passed. When it grew dark outside, they sat around the fire watching the shadows flickering into the room.

Mac drew Tracy to one side of the fireplace a bit away from the others and circled her shoulders with his arm. "Scared?"

She shook her head. "Not really. I just feel sorry for our parents. They must be worried sick."

"Yeah, but there's nothing we can do. Let's think of other things."

"What other things?" She stared dreamily into the fire, resting her head on his shoulder.

"Us, for instance." Mac lowered his voice, making his words just for her. "I love you, Tracy." He pulled her closer to him. "Someday after we're married we'll have our own house with a fireplace, and on winter nights we'll sit around the hearth eating popcorn, drinking cider, listening to soft music. I can hardly wait, Tracy. You're everything I want in this world."

Tracy welcomed the physical comfort of Mac's nearness, but she felt awkward and uneasy. She didn't want to hurt him, but she couldn't return his compliment. Not honestly. She couldn't tell him he was all she wanted in the world because it wasn't true. She wanted him, but she also wanted to go to college. She wanted a law degree. And she knew he wasn't being totally honest with himself.

"Mac, I'm not really *all* you want. You want a career in archaeology. Don't deny that."

"You're the only *girl* I want, Tracy. You know what I mean."

"And you're the only boy I want, Mac."

She could say that honestly enough. And she could return Mac's light kiss honestly enough, too.

"Say you'll marry me in June, Tracy. I want to hear you say the words."

"You promised me I had until Easter to make the final decision," she reminded him. "Please don't crowd me, Mac. I love you so much, but . . ."

"We'll be married in the church — a big wedding with you in white satin and me in a tux and we'll have lots of bridesmaids and groomsmen standing up with us — if that's what you want. Then we'll drive to Arizona for the big dig the university's sponsoring this summer. I've already signed up and I've reserved housing in the married students' unit."

"What will I do while you're working on the dig?"

"Oh, you'll find plenty to keep you busy. There'll be other wives. You can coffee with them during the day; then at night we'll be together."

Tracy snuggled closer to Mac just as Mrs. Sterling spoke from the other side of the fireplace.

"I think we should bank the fire now and get to bed, kids."

"But it's early, Mom," Jill said.

"I know, but there's no more hope of rescue today, and we'll want to be up early in the morning. Maybe we can work out some way to signal for help. Even after the main highway is open we're going to have to figure out some way to let people know we're here."

Reluctantly Jill stood, walked over to Tracy, and offered her a hand.

"Your mom's right, Jill," Mac said. "Since we don't have enough food, we're going to have to sleep or we won't have any energy at all." Mac rose and helped Tom put out the fire before they all trooped upstairs.

"Want me to sleep in your room again tonight?" Jill asked Tracy, her tone hinting that she really didn't want to.

"I'll be okay, Jill. You keep your mother company. I'm not going to have another nightmare."

"Okay, if you're sure."

"I'm sure."

Tracy removed her boots since her feet were fairly warm, but she left her clothes on. Would her navy outfit ever be the same again? Could the dry cleaners work miracles on it? The thought left her mind as other more important worries flooded in. But Mac was right. There was no use worrying about her parents or her job, so she put those things out of her mind, too. And that left Mac for her to think about. Mac and their engagement. Their June wedding.

She loved Mac. She was sure of that. And when she was near him, hearing his sure, confident voice paint lovely word pictures of their wedding, she knew she wanted to be married in June. She closed her eyes and imagined organ music, imagined herself walking down the aisle, her arm linked through her father's. But when she opened her eyes and saw only dark, cold reality, she began to have inner doubts.

Did she want to spend the rest of her life "coffeeing" with other wives? It sounded like dullsville. It sounded as Victorian as this very house — an old-fashioned place that offered protection, but no real freedom. She had the crazy feeling that if she married Mac in June she would be taking a step into the past instead of a step into the future. She pulled a blanket over her head and tried not to think at all.

• 5 •

Tracy had no idea what time it was when she heard somebody calling her name. At first it sounded like her mother, and she thought she had been dreaming. Then the voice grew slightly louder, more insistent, and she knew she wasn't dreaming. Someone was here, right here in the room with her. She opened her eyes while lying perfectly still, and for a moment she saw nothing but the dark of the room. Then she sensed a dim glow moving at the side of her bed.

"Are you awake, Tracy?"

Tracy pretended not to hear. Was she dreaming? This time she had to be sure whether or not she was dreaming. No. No dream. She was awake and she was quite aware of what was going on. She was in bed with all her clothes on — all except her boots — and she was almost warm, but not quite. And she was hungry, so hungry that her stomach was growling. She blinked, hoping the apparition of Victoria Graydon would disappear. But it didn't.

"I know you're awake, Tracy. I can sense that you are. I can tell about things like that. Please talk to me. Please help me."

Digging her heels into the mattress, Tracy pushed to a sitting position and then pulled the covers up around her neck as she faced Victoria Graydon. The girl was wearing the same pale lilac dress she had worn the night before. Her hair still flowed to her waist and her face still held the sad, troubled expression. Tracy wanted to call Mac just to show him that Victoria was actually present, but she was afraid to, afraid Victoria would disappear again, leaving her looking ridiculous in Mac's eyes.

"How can I help you?" Tracy held her voice to a whisper, telling herself she was doing it consciously. Yet she knew she was so scared she couldn't have spoken any louder had she wanted to. "I mean, I don't even know how to talk to a ... a ..."

"Ghost?" Victoria asked. "As long as you can see me you can talk to me just as you would talk to any person. I want to be your friend, Tracy."

Tracy squirmed, wondering what to say or do.

Victoria smiled at her. "May I sit down beside you?"

Mutely Tracy nodded and watched as Victoria sat on the edge of the bed without causing the least bit of movement in the mattress. In fact, Tracy could see right through Victoria to the blanket beneath her.

"Will you help me?" Victoria asked. "I think you can, if you will."

"I don't even understand what's troubling you." Tracy felt very self-conscious about talking with a ghost, a person she could see right through.

"I'd like to tell you about the things that are bothering me," Victoria said. "Will you listen?"

Tracy nodded once more. Listening would be easier than talking. And if this long-ago girl had really murdered her sister, maybe she only needed to confess to put herself at rest. Hadn't she read that someplace? Sometimes the dead person couldn't rest if she had a guilty conscience. Maybe that was Victoria's trouble.

"I'll start at the beginning," Victoria said. "I'm glad that you're in love, Tracy, because that should help you to understand how I feel."

"How do you know I'm in love?"

"I watched you with Mac. I heard your talk."

"You were spying on us?" Tracy felt like telling Victoria to get out of her life, but fright made her hold her temper.

"I wasn't spying. I just couldn't help *knowing* how it is between you and Mac. Coming back to walk among the living is no ordinary thing with me. You see, Rowena died just one hundred years ago this week. A century ago. This is the first time since I died that I've been able to appear to anyone in your world."

"I see," Tracy said, not seeing at all.

"Years ago I was engaged to Zachary Hawkins. He farmed the section next to this one and he was tall and blond and very handsome. He was my life, Tracy. He was everything to me. I loved him the same way you love your Mac."

"Did you marry him?" Maybe she can give me some advice, Tracy thought, suddenly more interested than she cared to admit.

"No. Zachary and I never married." Victoria stared into the distance. "Rowena stole him from me." Victoria looked back at Tracy, scowling. "She did it just for spite. She was jealous of me. It was that way from the minute I was born. Everything I had, Rowena wanted. Only she didn't really love Zachary, not at all. She just wanted to take him away from me."

"Are you sure?"

"Rowena was two years old when I was born," Victoria said. "Nanny told me that Rowena resented me from birth."

"Nanny?"

"Nanny. Our cook and housekeeper. My parents loved me, Tracy, but Nanny was the only person in the whole world who both loved me and understood me."

"I'm glad you had someone on your side." Tracy wished she had someone like Nanny.

She really could empathize with Victoria. Her parents loved her, but they didn't understand her. She couldn't seem to talk over her problems about Mac with them. Whenever Tracy tried, her mother said the marriage decision was up to her. She herself had married right out of high school and she had never regretted it. And her father also agreed that the decision would have to be Tracy's. Law was a fine career, but he couldn't make a career/marriage choice for her.

Tracy eased forward, not feeling as reluctant to talk with Victoria as she had a few minutes earlier. "How did Nanny try to help you, Victoria?"

"In lots of ways. I was so depressed. I suffered from terrible headaches whenever I thought of losing Zachary, which, of course, was all the time. Nanny gave me laudanum for my headaches and to soothe my mind. And she spent hours with me."

"What did you do during those hours?"

"Oh, she would talk with me, try to reason with me, tell me there were other men in the world and other fish in the sea. Nanny always said old-fashioned things like that. And she read to me from books and from her secret journal. She sometimes wrote poetry and she didn't let anyone but me read it."

"Ah, your nanny was a poet."

Victoria smoothed the skirt of her dress. "Yes, she was a poet, but nobody in the family knew it. Nobody except me, and I kept her secret. Nanny was a hard worker and she had had very little education. She thought people would laugh at her and think she was putting on airs if they found out she liked to write poetry."

"And did her poetry cheer you up?" Tracy asked, amazed to find herself almost eager to keep this strange conversation going.

"No." Victoria frowned again. "Nothing cheered me up. Nothing at all. I wished Rowena were dead. Every day and all day long I would keep saying in my mind that I wished my sister were dead."

"Victoria!"

"Please don't judge me. Instead, help me. I need help."

"I didn't mean to sound judgmental."

"Well, that's how you sounded, but I suppose I really can't blame you. I became almost as hateful a person as Rowena. I didn't like myself at all."

"Wishing a person dead won't make it happen," Tracy said. "But go ahead with your story."

"You're wrong." Victoria's voice grew so soft it was barely audible. "You're wrong about the wishing. On a night just like tonight our family was snowed in while a blizzard howled across this prairie land. But we weren't too worried about the storm. Papa had cared for the livestock and bedded all the critters in the barn. Mama had helped Nanny prepare us a good, warm supper.

Later, before we retired, Papa read to us from *Oliver Twist*. Everything seemed normal, except for the blizzard, of course."

The look in Victoria's eyes both fascinated and repelled Tracy. It was a look of mingled hate and sadness. And it was an imploring look, too, an imploring look directed straight at her.

"The next morning Rowena was dead." Victoria spoke matter-of-factly, all the while staring at her hands folded in her lap. "This was Rowena's room. Mine was across the hall. On that morning I had gone downstairs for breakfast. Rowena seldom got up early, but when she wasn't downstairs by midmorning, Mama got worried and went to see if she was all right."

"And she was dead?"

"Yes. I had wished her dead and she had died."

"Victoria, that's crazy. People just can't wish other people dead and have their wish come true."

"I did."

"You didn't. You *couldn't* have. You're suffering needlessly from all this."

"There is more to my story, Tracy. The worst is yet to come."

Tracy couldn't imagine anything worse than the tale Victoria had already told. She pulled the blankets more tightly about her and sat quietly.

"I tried to make Nanny understand that I had wished Rowena dead, but Nanny wouldn't listen to such a tale. Nanny thought I could do no wrong. Of course, Papa called the doctor. By that time it had stopped snowing and the doctor hitched his team to his sleigh and made it to the house within an hour. But he could find no cause for Rowena's death. None at all."

"She must have eaten something that made her sick," said Tracy. "Or perhaps she had a heart attack. Sometimes young people do have attacks."

"There was *nothing* wrong with her. There was no indication that she had been harmed in any way. The doctor said her death came from natural causes and he listed heart failure on the death certificate."

"You should accept the doctor's word, Victoria. His signature on the death certificate should settle the matter."

"Think about it, Tracy. Everyone dies of heart failure in the last analysis, don't they?"

"I suppose they do at that." Tracy wondered how she was ever going to think of something to say that would make Victoria feel better.

"After the doctor left I became hysterical. I knew I had murdered Rowena and I couldn't live with the knowledge. Mama and Papa tried to comfort me. Of course they didn't believe what I was saying. They thought Rowena's death had pushed me over the edge into insanity. And Nanny tried to comfort me, too. She was almost as distraught as I was and, and ..."

". . . and?" Tracy asked as Victoria began breathing in short, shallow gasps. "Go on, please go on."

"And Nanny had a heart attack and died on the spot. I killed her, too, Tracy. Nanny, the only one who loved and understood me. She was so distraught over my feeling guilty about Rowena that she had a heart attack. I can still remember her last words."

Victoria wiped her eyes and swallowed her tears; then she spoke again.

"I'll never forget Nanny's words, Tracy. Even to the end she was my friend. She said, 'You didn't will Rowena's death with your wishing, Victoria. That's quite impossible. In my journal . . .' Then her voice trailed off. That's all she said. Those were her very last words. She was thinking of me right until the end. Can you understand how I felt, Tracy? In that moment I knew I was responsible for both Rowena's and Nanny's deaths. It was more than I could bear. I withdrew into a shell and stopped talking to people. I couldn't even talk to Mama and Papa. And I couldn't eat. I soon died, too, but even death didn't free me of my guilt. My spirit keeps coming back to Rowena's room, back to this house, trying to find peace of mind and soul. But still such peace eludes me."

"I'm sorry, Victoria." The words sounded weak in Tracy's ears, yet she could think of nothing else to say to this ghost girl.

"If you're really sorry, you'll say you'll try to help me," Victoria pleaded.

"But I don't know what I can do to help."

"Just say you'll try. Just tell me you'll try to help me before this anniversary week ends."

Tracy closed her eyes, unable to bear the sight of Victoria's sad face. "All right, Victoria. I'll try to help you. I really will."

When Tracy opened her eyes, ready to listen to suggestions from Victoria on just *how* she might be of help, she found herself alone in the room once more.

· 6 ·

Victoria?" Tracy called the name softly. No
reply. She called again. "Victoria?" Still no
answer. Maybe the ghost girl was gone for
good. In a way Tracy hoped so, but in another
way she hoped not. She had promised to try
to help her, hadn't she? How could she help
someone who was dead? Did Victoria's ab-
sence cancel out the promise? Tracy knew
it didn't. She stretched out in the bed again;
then she curled into a ball and tried to get
warm. It was a long time before she dropped
off to sleep.

Sun shining through her window awakened
Tracy the next morning. Mac was calling to
her from the head of the stairway. For a moment she didn't open her eyes. How could she
bear to face this day?

"Hey, Tracy. Wake up. The blizzard's over.
The snow's stopped."

Tracy opened her eyes, but she didn't jump

up. "Coming," she called. She heard Mac's step thumping downstairs, but still she didn't throw the covers back. She had to reach a few decisions first. But after a little thought she realized the decisions weren't all that hard to make. She simply was not going to mention a word about seeing Victoria again. No use getting everyone all upset about ghosts.

Having made that decision, Tracy flung the covers back and shivered as she watched her breath form white clouds in the frigid air. She combed her hair and put on some lip gloss. If only she could have a bath! She hurried downstairs where everyone was huddled around a newly laid fire Mac was trying to coax into being.

"More boards, Tom." Mac threw a stick of wood into the chimney. "Let's get enough wood on there to really put out some heat."

"Your wish is my command, good sir." Tom bowed from the waist and dropped four more boards onto the hearth.

Tracy stopped at the doorway into the living room and stared at her companions. Did she look as bad as the rest of them looked? Mrs. Sterling's suit was a mass of wrinkles, and her hair had lost its crisp curl. Today, Jill's blazer was missing one of its buttons, and her skirt sagged at the side seams and across the seat. The boys didn't exactly look like mannequins from a display window, either. Tom's hair always had a windblown look that was attractive, but today his chin was dark with unsightly stubble, and Mac's thick hair looked as if it might take a professional landscaping rather than a simple styling to get it back in shape. Tracy touched her own hair, felt strands clumping together and hanging over her ears. How she wished she had her herbal shampoo and her blow dryer.

"And what would Madam prefer for breakfast?" Mac asked Tracy. "Hot water or cold water?"

"What? No pork and beans? How can a girl face the day without pork and beans for breakfast?" Joking made her feel a little better, but not much. How long had she and Victoria talked last night? She still felt sleepy. Or maybe she was weak from hunger. She was just heading across the living room to try to look out the front window when the news announcer spoke. Today there was no static interference and his voice came in clearly.

"And here is the latest traveler's advisory. Although the snow has stopped, highways and city streets are still 100 percent blocked with snowdrifts. Emergency crews are trying to open lanes for ambulance, police, and firefighters. Drivers are advised to postpone all but emergency travel. Stay tuned . . ."

"We'll get out of here today, don't you think?" Jill asked. "I mean, we'll waste away to nothing if we spend another twenty-four hours here without any food."

"We still have one more can of beans," Mrs. Sterling said. "And part of a can of peaches."

"Do I look any thinner?" Jill asked.

"My, yes," Tom said. "You've changed right before our very eyes. Tell us about your diet. No, on second thought, just tell me, Jill. Maybe we can collaborate on a book — *The Iowa Blizzard Diet Book*. Catchy title, right?"

"Wrong," Jill said. Tracy laughed in spite of herself, thinking ruefully that they would be okay as long as they kept their sense of humor. She headed to the window again, pulling Mac along with her; then she turned, frowning. "The snowdrifts are completely covering the windows on this side of the house. I can't see the road at all. It must be worse out there than it was yesterday."

"So what's out there to see but snow and more snow?" Mac squeezed her hand and brushed a kiss against her cheek. "We'll probably never get to spend so much time together again until we're married."

Tracy smiled up at him. "You're right, Mac. We'll probably look back on this and appreciate all the time we've had together."

"How about helping me bring up some more wood, Mac?" Tom asked.

"Sure thing." Mac kissed his finger and touched it to Tracy's nose. "Be right back. Don't go away."

"I won't."

"Good. Don't ever leave me."

Tracy stared after Mac, thinking how loving he was.

"Since these windows are blocked, I'm going upstairs to look out," Tracy said to Jill, wishing she had looked out before she'd come downstairs. But she had been sleepy, and she had still been thinking about Victoria. Besides, she hadn't known snow was covering the lower windows.

"Just a sec and I'll come up with you," Jill said.

Tracy headed up the stairs, but when she reached the doorway of her bedroom she hesitated. What if Victoria was there? Why should she have to face the room again? Surely they would be out of this house at least by this afternoon. She would forget all about Victoria. If she could. That big word *if* again.

"Hey, where are you going?" Mac called to her, starting up the steps behind her.

"Yeah, wait up," Jill called.

"I'm going up to the third floor," Tracy said. "There should be a great view of the whole countryside from that high up."

"Jill? Mac?" Mrs. Sterling's voice called from the living room. "Come listen to this latest news bulletin. They're going to repeat it. Quick! Before it's over."

"Be right with you, Tracy," Mac called over his shoulder as he turned to go back downstairs.

Tracy opened the door to the third floor stairway and stared up. She sniffed. Again she imagined she smelled the faint aroma of pipe tobacco. She sniffed again and didn't smell it at all. My imagination, she thought. She ran up the short flight of stairs quickly and was almost at the top when she heard Mac call to her.

"Tracy, you've got to come down here and listen to this. It'll blow your mind. The guy on the radio is talking about us. Come on."

Tracy hesitated. The announcement, whatever it was, would be over before she could get downstairs. And it would no doubt be repeated later. She decided to go up and take a quick peek from the ballroom windows. She was just getting ready to turn to take the last few steps when she felt strong hands on her shoulders. She gasped as someone shoved her.

Frantically she clutched for a wall and then at air as she fell forward and tumbled down the stairs, banging her knees, her elbows, her head.

She fell into a blackness that surrounded her like soft cotton.

· 7 ·

Tracy! Tracy!"

Tracy heard someone shouting her name as if from the bottom of a deep well. She opened her eyes and looked up at Mac who was leaning over her. "What's the matter, Mac?" Then she realized that she was hurt. She hurt almost everywhere. She managed to lift her hand to her head where a great lump had formed. She looked at her fingers, surprised that they weren't bloody.

"What happened?" Jill flipped her ponytail over her shoulder. "Did you trip? We heard a terrible crash."

"Are you hurt?" Mac placed his cold hand on her forehead.

"I'm all right, I think. I hurt all over." Then memory returned. She wanted to jump up, but she couldn't. Allowing Mac and Mrs. Sterling to help her, she slowly rose to her feet and peered up the stairway. "But I didn't fall."

"No, of course not," Jill said. "Tracy, I think you hit your head harder than you think."

"Someone *pushed* me," Tracy said. "I was almost at the top of the steps when I heard Mac call me. I had turned and started to come down, and then I decided to go up for a quick look out the window. *Someone on the third floor pushed me down the stairs.*"

"Let's take a look up there," Mac said. "Maybe we're not the only ones who broke into this house. Maybe someone has been hiding up there all along. That might explain those crackers we found."

He and Tom took the steps two at a time, ready to do battle. When all remained quiet, Jill, Tracy, and Mrs. Sterling followed the boys. Tracy felt shaky and wobbly. Every muscle ached, but she refused to stay behind.

"Watch out, Mac," she called. "Someone's up there." Her heart pounded and she felt sweat on her forehead. Sweat! In this cold house!

"I don't see anyone," Mac said.

"But look at all these footprints in the dust." Tom pointed. "Someone's been up here."

"Of course," Jill said. "That's no mystery. Tracy and Mac explored this floor yesterday."

Tracy nodded, doubting that her voice would work.

"Let's take a look behind those doors at each end of the room." Tom strode to the door Mac and Tracy had opened the day before, and after struggling to get it open he found the same thing they had found. Nothing.

"What about the other door?" Tom said. He jogged to it and pulled. "Hey! It's locked or something."

"Let me try." Mac joined him and lifted on the latch, but the door didn't give. He pulled, but still the door didn't budge. "It doesn't seem to be locked." He stood back studying it.

"We had a hard time opening that other door," Tracy said. "But it was just stuck."

"It's probably swollen from all the damp and cold," Mrs. Sterling said. "But if we can't get it open from this side, then nobody can get it open from the other side, either."

"Yeah." Mac looked at Tracy for a moment, then glanced away as if he were embarrassed.

"Tracy," Jill said. "It's clear that there's nobody up here. And nobody could have come downstairs without being seen. You must have imagined that someone pushed you."

"I didn't imagine it." Tracy felt her hands clench into fists.

"I know you don't think you imagined it, dear," Mrs. Sterling said. "But I know we're all weak from hunger. It would have been easy for you to have slipped on the steps.

And lack of food can do strange things to one's thinking."

"But ..." Tracy spluttered.

"Let's go downstairs now and just be glad you didn't break any bones."

Tracy allowed Mrs. Sterling to persuade her to go back downstairs, but she knew she had been pushed. She was dismayed that Mac didn't believe her. If she couldn't depend on Mac, then who could she depend on?

They gathered around the fireplace and Mac heated up their last can of pork and beans. Tracy decided to keep quiet about her fall. At least she wasn't bleeding. She sat nursing her aching muscles and her bruised knees and elbows.

The leaping flames almost hypnotized her. Who had pushed her? Victoria? But could a girl who sat on the edge of a bed without moving the mattress actually push someone down a flight of stairs? And Victoria had no reason to push her. She had said she wanted to be her friend. It made no sense to think Victoria had shoved her.

"What are you thinking, Tracy?" Jill asked as she offered Tracy a small helping of the beans.

"Nothing." Tracy accepted the beans without comment. She was glad Victoria had explained about Rowena's death, or at least explained her part in it. Tracy was sure a person could not wish another person dead. The ghost girl who had sat on her bed was not a murderess. She would try to hold that thought. Victoria was a girl in need of help.

"Eat, Tracy," Mrs. Sterling urged. "It's not much, but you'll get some strength from even a little food. Beans are mostly protein. Good, substantial fare."

"I'm going outside," Mac said. "I found a shovel in the cellar. I'm going to try to dig a path to the car."

"What for?" Tom asked. "The battery will be dead."

"Yeah, suppose so. Guess I'm just getting stir crazy. I'd like to get a whiff of fresh air and a touch of that sunshine."

"Yeah, and a snootful of that snow." Tom groaned, but he decided to go with Mac.

After the boys were outside and after Mrs. Sterling had gone upstairs to see that all the bedrooms were in order, Jill leaned close to Tracy.

"You didn't see that ghost girl again last night, did you?"

Tracy felt a chill feather up her arm at Jill's question and she evaded it. "I slept well last night. No nightmares. I was good and warm when I went to bed — even my feet. I really konked out."

"I didn't ask how you slept. I asked if you saw Victoria again—in a dream, I mean."

Tracy was about to tell an out-and-out lie when the radio which Mac had left on the table drew her attention. "Listen, Jill, they just said our names."

"I heard all that on an earlier broadcast.

That's what I wanted you to come down for. They keep giving the same news."

"Then let me listen now, okay?" Tracy walked to the radio and stood listening.

". . . five people still reported missing. Mrs. Claudia Sterling, her daughter Jill, and three other students, Tracy Pendelton, Tom Crendal, and Mac Gordon were last seen leaving the music auditorium on the Drake University campus. Mrs. Sterling was driving a cream-colored Chevrolet Citation, license number ECK 308 Marshall County. Anyone knowing or learning the whereabouts of these people, please contact either the radio station or the police."

"Don't you know our parents are just dying of worry!" Tracy thrust her fists deep into her jacket pockets, but before she could say more, the radio announcer continued.

". . . hay is being airlifted from Des Moines and Cedar Rapids to Marshall County, which is the area hardest hit by the blizzard. Cattlemen desiring hay for their livestock may call the following number —"

"An airlift!" Tracy exclaimed.

"What good's that going to do us? Unless, of course, you'd like a bale of alfalfa for lunch."

"Airplanes, Jill. If planes are overhead, maybe some pilot will see smoke from our fire and investigate."

"And not even realize this house is deserted. The pilots will be from Des Moines or Cedar Rapids. They won't think it's strange to see smoke coming from a chimney."

"It's a chance, and I think we should build up the fire and put out all the smoke we can."

They were still adding boards to the fireplace grate when Mac and Tom slammed back inside, bringing a blast of cold air with them. They stamped snow from their feet and brushed snow from their clothes.

"Who's going to donate a scarf for the cause?" Mac asked.

"What cause?" Tracy asked. "But if your ears are freezing you can use mine." She looked around the room and then remembered she had left her scarf upstairs.

"It's not for our ears," Mac said. "I think we can dig out to the car and tie a scarf onto the radio antenna. Maybe someone will see it and look for us."

"There's a hay airlift underway," Tracy said, interrupting. "Maybe some pilot might see a scarf at that. Good idea, Mac! We can't get out of here soon enough to suit me. I'll go get my scarf."

"Better take mine." Jill picked her scarf up from the sofa. "It's red and yours is navy blue. Mine would be easier to see."

"You're right." Mac took the scarf from her and the boys went back outside. Tracy would have liked to have watched them, but she wasn't about to go upstairs again. In only a few moments Mrs. Sterling joined Tracy and Jill by the fire, and almost immediately

Mac and Tom blustered back inside, again filling the room with cold air.

"What's the matter?" Tracy eyed Jill's scarf still dangling from Mac's hand.

"The wind's blowing so hard that the trail we had cleared is covered with snow. We've got to rest awhile before we can do any more shoveling."

For a moment nobody spoke, but Tracy knew the same thought was in all their minds. If the wind was still blowing that hard, then the maintenance crews would be unable to clear the highways effectively. Mac turned up the volume on the radio, and Tracy heard their fears voiced.

"Highways and streets are covered with drifting snow. All snow-clearing operations are being halted until the wind subsides. Snowmobiles are still providing service in emergency situations. If you need help, please call this radio station or dial 911. And stay tuned to keep abreast of the latest storm developments. We are here to serve you."

"I'd like to see them serve me a quarter-pounder and a large order of fries and . . ."

"Cork it, Tom," Mac said. "We may as well face the fact. We're stranded here for another day. The less we think about food, the better off we'll be."

"We still have some peaches," Mrs. Sterling said. "I guess that'll be our lunch."

"Better than no lunch at all," Mac said.

Tracy said nothing. How could she bear to spend another night here? She might have been killed in that fall. Someone had shoved her. She was *sure*. And what if Victoria showed up again? She hadn't kept her promise to try to help Victoria. She couldn't even think of a way she might begin to help her. And she ached all over.

She stood and headed for the sofa, hurting with every step. Maybe she could sleep away some of the time. Easing down gently, she curled into a ball, resting her head on a velvet cushion.

"Don't go to sleep, Tracy," Mrs. Sterling said.

"But I'm so tired."

"You did hit your head in that fall." Mrs. Sterling walked to her, took her hand, and insisted that she stand. "When Jill had a head injury several years ago, the doctor made her keep on her feet and walk for at least two hours. I think that's what you should do. I feel so responsible. I wouldn't want you to have any problems because we didn't do the right thing for you."

"Walk for two hours here in the house?" Tracy wanted to argue, but she didn't. She was too tired.

"Of course. You can walk from the front door to the back door. You can walk upstairs and back downstairs and even to the cellar if you want to." Mrs. Sterling gave her an encouraging smile.

"Come on," Mac said. "I'll walk with you. It keeps the blood circulating."

"Okay. For a while." She confined her

walking to the first floor of the house. She and Mac walked around each room, examining everything carefully. She studied the dishes in the china closet.

"Like them?" Mac asked.

"Yeah. They're pretty, but they're sort of plain."

"When are we going to choose our dishes? You know, the ones people will give us for wedding gifts?"

"Mac, please don't rush me. It's too soon to be thinking about that. We haven't even announced our engagement yet." Tracy crossed the room, examining the books on the sideboard. Surely that was neutral ground. Nothing there to start an argument.

Mac walked with her the whole two hours, and she felt guilty about her earlier irritation at him as she realized he really must care about her. Surely he wanted to sit down and rest as much as she did. But he was sticking by her. She found his help very comforting. It was easier to face being stranded with Mac at her side. While they were still walking she had an idea that she thought might help them, but she waited until Mrs. Sterling let her sit down before she mentioned it.

"I really don't think any pilot is going to consider smoke rising from a chimney a distress signal." She dropped onto the floor near the fireplace. "But we could rig up a signal a pilot *would* notice."

"How?" Mac asked. "And what?"

"Yeah," Tom said. "What sort of a signal?

I suppose we could run out whenever we heard a plane. Wave. Shout."

"Negative," Mac said. "The pilot might not spot us. What's your idea, Tracy?"

"We could take our blankets, roll them lengthwise, and carry them outside. Then we could lay them on the snow and form the letters SOS. Any pilot would know that was a distress signal."

"Hey, all right!" Mac said. "I think it might work."

Tom slapped Tracy on the back, but she ignored him as she looked at Mac who was smiling broadly.

Tom started upstairs. "Come on, gang. Let's get the blankets."

"Wait." Mrs. Sterling's tone stopped Tom, and everyone gave her their attention. "I don't think you should use the blankets in the snow, kids. Think. No matter how carefully you roll them, they're going to get wet."

"Yeah." Jill's shoulders slumped. "If we have to sleep here again, well, who wants a wet blanket?"

They all sat by the fire again, and then Mac spoke up. "We could use the curtains and draperies instead of the blankets. How about that?"

"We shouldn't destroy property that isn't ours," Tracy said. "Those draperies are so rotten they'll shred at the touch."

"But we're starving," Jill said.

"And there aren't many cellar shelves left," Mac said. "When they're gone, we're going to have to start burning furniture if we don't want to freeze."

"I suppose that would be worse that damaging the draperies," Tracy admitted. "The draperies are rotten anyway."

"What's going to keep the wind from blowing the draperies away once we get them in place?" Tom asked.

"We are," Mac said. "Come on, little buddy. There must be some rocks or something outside that we can use for weights. We'll go find something while you all take down the draperies."

"Good idea," Mrs. Sterling said.

"Bring the shovel, Tom." Mac started out the door. "We'll probably have to do some digging."

The boys went outside again, and Tracy began eyeing the draperies. "Which ones shall we use?"

"The darkest ones," Jill said. "They'll show up best against snow."

"The ones in the boys' bedroom are dark green," Mrs. Sterling said. "I'll take them down while you girls work on the ones in this room, okay?"

Jill and Tracy dragged an oak chair to a window. Jill stood on it, examining the drapery hooks and the rods, sneezing as dust rose from the old fabric. They pulled up another chair, and Tracy tried to hold her breath as she worked, turning her head away from the dust whenever she could.

"You're awfully quiet, Tracy," Jill said.

"Are you feeling okay? No headache or anything?"

"I'm fine." Tracy dropped the draperies she had been working on in a heap, wondering how big the letters were going to have to be, so they would be visible from the sky. Jill chattered as they worked, and Tracy hadn't realized that she had been answering her in monosyllables until Jill stopped and looked at her with a direct gaze.

"Tracy, what's the matter? Did you have nightmares about that ghost girl again last night? I can tell something's bothering you, and if it wasn't the fall, then what is it? You don't believe that ghost girl is real, do you? You don't think that she appeared and, and pushed you ... do you?"

· 8 ·

Tracy sighed. She and Jill had been best friends for years and they seldom kept secrets from each other, yet she hesitated, not sure she wanted to tell Jill about what had gone on in her room the night before.

"You *did* see her, didn't you?" Jill demanded.

Tracy dusted her hands against her skirt and set the dining room chairs back in place. "Yes, I did see her, Jill. And I wasn't dreaming. I didn't imagine it. Victoria was in my room. She talked to me. We talked together and I promised to help her."

"Help her!"

Tracy clamped her teeth together and began picking up the draperies.

"I'm sorry," Jill apologized. "If you say you saw Victoria I believe you saw her. But *help* her? I know you're a soft touch for anyone in trouble, but how can you help a ghost?"

"I'll tell you what she told me last night if you promise not to laugh."

"Promise."

"Not even a smile."

"Promise."

Tracy took a deep breath; then she sighed, trying to find just the right place to start her story. She finally decided to tell it exactly as it happened. True to her promise, Jill didn't laugh or even smile, but when Tracy finished the tale, Jill shook her head.

"I don't see how you're going to help a ghost prove she didn't murder her sister. And that's what she wants, Tracy. She may not come right out and say so, but I think she wants you to convince her that she didn't kill Rowena and that she didn't cause her nanny's heart attack."

"I don't know how I can help. I certainly don't know what went on here a hundred years ago."

"There's no way you can help. So forget it." Then Jill paused thoughtfully and after a few moments said, "Tracy, you don't think, I mean, you don't really believe that the ghost of Victoria Graydon pushed you down the stairs just as sort of a threat, do you? You know, sort of a reminder of what might happen if you *don't* help?"

"No."

"But how can you be so sure?"

Tracy knew there was no way she could convince Jill that she had felt human hands shoving her, no way that she could convince her that Victoria could touch things without so much as disturbing them even slightly.

"That fall could have killed me, Jill." Tracy heard her voice waver as she spoke the truth she hated to face. "Why would someone who wanted me to help her try to *hurt* me? That just doesn't make any sense at all, does it?"

"How can you stand there and spout logical questions about such an illogical happening? *None* of this makes sense, you know."

"Will you try to help me help Victoria?"

Jill walked to the window and peered outside for many moments before she answered. "No, Tracy. I'm not going to try to help. Frankly, I think you dreamed this ghost and I think you stumbled down the stairs. I know everything seemed real to you, but the things you're saying just aren't logical."

Tracy tried to cork her anger, to keep her voice normal. It wouldn't help matters any to be at odds with Jill. But if Jill wanted logic, she could give her some. "Jill, you're one of the people who didn't want to come to this house because you thought it was haunted, remember? Yet when a ghost appears, you don't believe it. *You're* the one who's not making sense."

"The ghost didn't appear to *me*." Jill scowled; then she hurried to Tracy's side. "If a ghost had appeared to me I would have gone bananas. I mean it. Completely bananas. I would have had a fit. I guess I don't want to believe your story because if I believed it, I would be so scared I couldn't cope. Does that make sense to you?"

"Not too much. I'm sorry, Jill. I suppose it does make sense in a way. If you can deny that a thing exists, then you don't have to cope with it, do you?"

"Right. It may be the coward's way out, but for right now, just color me yellow."

Before Tracy and Jill could say anything more, Mrs. Sterling came downstairs dragging two dark draperies behind her.

"I can't bear to pick them up, they're so dusty. Now, how are we going to keep them in long, thin cylinders?"

"I saw a string ball in the kitchen," Tracy said. "We could tie them." She ran to the kitchen and got the string.

"Bet it's rotten," Jill said.

Tracy tested it. It broke easily, but it was sturdy enough for their purpose. Mrs. Sterling and Jill stretched the draperies lengthwise on the dining room floor and rolled them into long cylinders while Tracy tied them in place with the string. They were almost finished when Mac and Tom returned.

"Did you find enough rocks?" Mrs. Sterling asked. "It's going to take quite a few."

"We didn't find any rocks," Mac said. "But we found a stack of bricks in that shed near the outhouse. We can form the letters near that shed so we won't have to carry the bricks very far."

"No way," Tracy said. "We should form

the letters in the middle of the yard. That way a pilot would be more likely to see them."

"Tracy's right," Jill said.

"Okay," Mac agreed. "But toting a bunch of bricks is going to be some job with that wind still howling the way it is."

"This is really some adventure," Tom said. "Just think of the story all this is going to make. And I'm not going to let some reporter from the *Times Republican* scoop me, either."

"How are you going to prevent that?" Mrs. Sterling asked, smiling.

"It may not be easy. But just as soon as we get those letters in place I'm going to start writing my own story. Then when we're rescued I'll just hand my story to the city editor myself." Tom stared into the distance. "FIVE SURVIVE BLIZZARD. I can see the headlines now."

"We haven't survived yet," Mac reminded him.

"Yeah," Jill said. "If you really want to write a story that'll attract some attention you'd better write up the one Tracy just told me."

"About falling down the stairs? Nobody's going to believe she was pushed." Tom looked at Tracy. "Sorry, but it's true."

"That wasn't the story I meant," Jill said. "I meant the *ghost* story. Tracy saw Victoria again. Last night."

"You weren't supposed to tell, Jill." Tracy heard her voice grow tight with disappointment and anger.

"You didn't *say* not to tell." Jill's chin jutted defiantly.

"Come on, Tracy," Tom said. "Give. No fair holding out on your friends. What happened?"

Tracy looked at Mac, trying to read his expression. He was holding himself very still in his quiet, thoughtful way, and his blue eyes were meeting hers in a way she didn't understand. Or maybe she did understand. He was looking at her in a way that begged her not to say anything that would embarrass him. In that moment Tracy knew she wasn't going to say any more about Victoria Graydon.

"Come on, Tracy," Tom begged. "Don't keep us in suspense."

"It wasn't anything." Tracy turned from the others and walked into the kitchen, but she could still hear them talking.

"What's with her?" Tom asked softly. "It's not like Tracy to play hard to get with anyone."

"I think we'd better drop the subject of ghosts," Mrs. Sterling said. "Tracy is just keyed up from hunger and worry. And I'm sure her fall gave her a real jolt. I'm going to urge her parents to take her to the doctor for a checkup as soon as we get out of here."

"I'll go talk to her." Mac laughed quietly. "It's not like Tracy to go bonkers over a ghost story. I'll see if I can reason with her."

Tracy wished she hadn't heard Mac's words. If Mac was against her, she simply couldn't bear it. She would have believed *him*, had he been the one to have claimed to have seen a ghost. She would have, wouldn't she? It was an easy thing to think she would have, but when she considered all that had happened to her from Mac's viewpoint she could understand his position, his doubting. People who were in their right minds didn't see ghosts. And if they stumbled down the stairs, they admitted it. She could empathize with Mac and was able to smile at him when he approached her.

"Tracy?" The word was a question, and when he held out his arms to her she rushed into them. A shelter. A haven.

"Mac!" He kissed her and held her tight, and for those few moments in his arms she could believe that things were all right. She could depend on Mac. Mac would protect her from all harm. She pulled away from him gently.

"Why do you keep on with this ghost business?" Mac asked, still holding her close with an arm around her waist. "You're going to scare Jill to death if you don't stop it."

"You don't believe me, do you?"

"Do you really expect me to?" Mac tilted her chin with his forefinger until she had to look directly into his penetrating gaze. "I don't understand you, Tracy. What proof can you offer?"

Tracy eased away from Mac. She had been ready to accept the fact that he didn't believe her story, but she couldn't accept knowing that he didn't understand her. That was another thing entirely.

"Maybe you aren't trying to understand me."

"What's that supposed to mean?"

She heard anger curl the edge of his voice like frost might curl a maple leaf. "I meant just what I said. I don't think you're *trying* to understand me, and if two people are really in love, then they try to understand each other. They try to relate to each other's opinions."

"I'm a *scientist*, Tracy. You simply can't expect me to believe in ghosts or to believe that you saw one."

"Are you a scientist before you're a human being?"

"What's *that* supposed to mean?"

"Why do you keep asking that? I think I made myself very clear." Without waiting for Mac to answer and without giving him a chance to touch her again, she brushed past him and joined the others in the living room. She could forgive the others for their doubt, but she couldn't forgive Mac for both doubt and lack of understanding. If they were going to spend the rest of their lives together, they were going to have to believe in and understand each other, weren't they?

Suddenly Tracy felt tears stinging behind her eyelids. Was she going to let a ghost come between her and the boy she loved, the boy she intended to marry? She kept her gaze down, looking into the fire so the others wouldn't see the tears. Now was no time for crying. She had already made enough of a fool of herself before her friends. She was still staring into the flames when they all heard a low, distant droning.

"Hey!" Mac shouted. "A plane. Listen!"

Everyone listened for an instant or two, and then Mac headed for the back door. "Come on, you guys. Let's get out there and wave like crazy. Maybe the pilot will see us. Hurry!"

They tumbled from the house like apples spilling from a basket, and Tracy was glad that the plane had distracted their attention from her. She coughed as she inhaled the frigid air, and her eyes watered so much that the whiteness around her blurred until it seemed like the whole world was a frozen cloud and her tears were the only warm thing in it. She looked up but couldn't even see the plane. She lurched forward into a deep drift, and snow sifted over her boot tops, easing down to her ankles like cold, wet fingers. Tom fell as he tried to help Tracy up, and they both looked like snowmen once they regained their footing.

"Wave, everyone!" Mac shouted. "Wave!" He raised both arms above his head and waved both hands back and forth as he stumbled through the drifts.

"Hey, up there!" Tom shouted as he waved. "Hey, up there!"

"He can't hear you," Mac said. "He can't hear anything but the plane engine."

"Maybe he's a she." Jill waved her red scarf. "Who says all pilots are men?"

"Are you kidding?" Mac guffawed at the idea. "Keep waving!"

They all waved and shouted, but the pilot didn't dip his wings or circle or give any other sign that he had seen them. At last they stopped trying to get his attention and plodded back to the house. Nobody said anything as they stood warming themselves at the fire, listening to the burning boards pop and hiss.

"Don't feel too bad, kids," Mrs. Sterling said at last.

"Sure, Mom." Jill shook snow from her red scarf. "We don't feel bad. It'll be lots of fun to stay here another night. I've been looking forward to it all day."

"And don't be sarcastic," her mother said. "That pilot will probably be coming back this way sometime soon. If we get the SOS signal out there he may see it on his return trip. Nobody said anything about staying here another night."

"Your mom's right," Tracy said. "The pilot will have to go back to home base before long. The airfields around here will be snow-covered."

"Then let's haul these draperies outside," Mac said. "I think the center of the front yard would be a good place for them. Over on the north side where there aren't any trees."

"Let's go," Tom said. "What are we waiting for?"

"Tracy, where's your scarf?" Mrs. Sterling asked. "You shouldn't go out there again without it. We'll probably be out longer this time. You could freeze your ears."

"It's upstairs." Tracy hated the thought of going upstairs for any reason.

"Go get it," Mrs. Sterling said.

"I'll go with you." Mac took her hand as she hesitated.

Tracy's face grew hot and she knew she was blushing, but she was glad that their fight was over and that Mac had offered to go upstairs with her. He held her hand tightly as they walked up the steps and along the hallway to the room where she had slept.

"Where is it?" Mac asked as they stepped through the doorway.

"On the dresser, I think." She looked on the dresser, but there was nothing there except the yellowed newspaper and the burned-down nub of a red candle in its tin jar lid. Tracy glanced around.

"Hey, there it is on the bed," Mac said.

A sudden feeling of foreboding froze Tracy to the spot, and she felt her nails dig into Mac's hand as she squeezed it.

"Hey! What's the big idea!" Mac pulled his hand free and rubbed it on the palm of his other hand.

"I didn't leave the scarf on the bed."

"Then how did it get there?" Mac stepped

toward the bed, but Tracy grabbed his arm, pulling him back.

"I know I straightened the bed covers and there was nothing on them when I left the room."

"Maybe you dropped the scarf. Maybe Jill picked it up. What difference does it make? Grab it and let's go."

Of course. Grab it and go. Mac's words made sense. Before he could step to the bed, she eased in front of him and snatched up the scarf. And as she did so a piece of paper fluttered to the floor.

"You dropped something," Mac said.

Tracy shook as she stooped to pick up the paper. She knew before she looked that there was going to be a message on it. That was the kind of thing that happened in a haunted house, wasn't it? She was glad Mac was with her. He would have to believe this was happening if he saw it, wouldn't he? And this time it wouldn't be just her word against everyone else's disbelief.

She turned the paper over and they read the message together.

Get out before it's too late. You are in danger.

· 9 ·

Tracy's hand shook so badly that Mac took
the scrap of paper from her so they could
examine it more closely. She didn't need to
look at it a second time. The words were
etched in her brain. First she was shoved.
Now she had been warned. Someone was
after her. But who? And why her? She
wanted to run from this horror of a house
and never think about it again.

"Looks like some little kid wrote it," Mac
said. "The printing's all scrawled in pencil
and sort of smeared."

"There aren't any little kids around here."

"What's the hang-up, you two?" Jill called
from the foot of the stairs. "Can't you find
the scarf?"

"We found it," Mac called. "And we found
something else, too. Better take a look."

Relief flooded through Tracy as she realized Mac wasn't laughing at her this time.
And why should he laugh? A note was a
tangible thing a person could touch and see.
By the time they had run downstairs the

others were waiting by the post. Mac thrust the note at them as he took Tracy's hand. They waited for a reaction.

"Who did this?" Mrs. Sterling frowned as her direct gaze met each of theirs in turn. "Which one of you is trying to be funny?"

No reply. In the silence Tracy heard the wind howl around the corners of the house, shaking the windowpanes.

"Tom?" Mrs. Sterling impaled Tom with her gaze. "You're the writer in the group. Do you know anything about this note?"

"Hey! No way!"

"Mom!" Jill stepped to Tom's side. "You're being unfair."

"Well, maybe so, but I think that under the circumstances this joke is in very poor taste." She looked at Tom. "I'm sorry I accused you, Tom. That *was* unfair of me." Nobody spoke as Mrs. Sterling walked to the fireplace and tossed the note into the flames. Tracy watched the paper brown at the edges, blacken, and disintegrate into gray black ash.

"Now, no more jokes," Mrs. Sterling said. "If anyone else has any more bright ideas, let's apply them to getting us home."

Tracy looked at each of the others, wondering in her heart if one of them had written the warning. Somebody had done it. That was for sure. And why had it been directed at her? It was almost as if the others in the house didn't matter, as if she were the only one in danger. But why? It made no sense.

Tracy thought about Mrs. Sterling's assumption. Was someone trying to play a joke? Jill? It could be. Jill disliked facing the reality of the ghostly visit from Victoria. What better way to deny it than to try to make a joke of it? Yet, would Jill really do that to her, knowing how seriously she had taken Victoria's appearance?

Tom? He had been Mrs. Sterling's first suspect. Sometimes Tom acted without thinking things through, yet she couldn't imagine him doing this. He was not that conservative with words. Tom talked a lot. And when he wrote, the words flowed. That note just wasn't in Tom's style. It was far too cryptic.

Mac? Tracy hated to think of that possibility. If Mac had done this to her she knew she would have a hard time forgiving him. But Mac wasn't a practical joker. She put the thought of Mac having written the note from her mind. She would rather have the guilty one be Tom or even Jill. But not Mac. She brightened a bit. Even she had accepted Mrs. Sterling's idea that the note was just someone's idea of a joke. And maybe she had slipped on the stairs. She wished she could believe that.

"Come on, kids," Mrs. Sterling said. "Lend a hand. Let's get the draperies outside."

"Yeah!" Mac agreed. "That pilot could return any minute."

Mac and Tom dragged all the draperies onto the porch while Tracy held the inside door and Jill propped the screen door out of the way. The wind had gone down some, but

Tracy felt it blow stinging snow into her face and whirl it down her coat collar.

"Everyone grab a drapery in each hand," Mac said, taking charge. "Don't try to lift them. Too heavy. Just drag them and follow me."

"You got it, man," Tom shouted.

Tracy willed this activity to fill her whole mind. She didn't want any brain cells left over that might dwell on her fall or on the warning. She tied her scarf tightly under her chin, grabbed a drapery in each hand, and plodded into the snow. How strange, she thought, that she could face the idea of talking with a ghost while the thought of her fall and the warning threw her for a loop.

"This way," Mac shouted and pointed.

They followed Mac to the north side of the yard where they began forming the letters, pushing and shaping the drapery fabric into a huge letter S.

"We need the bricks," Tracy said. "Come on, Jill. Let's go get a couple."

"We'd better all go," Mac said. "It's going to take more than four bricks to hold these letters down, and I don't think you girls can manage to carry more than one in each hand."

"I'll stay here and sit on the draperies to keep them from blowing into the next county," Mrs. Sterling said.

Mac linked his arm through Tracy's as they lowered their heads against the wind and pressed on toward the shed. Tracy's fingers already felt stiff and cold inside her mittens and she wished she were back by the fire. She could barely see the weathered, gray shed, it blended into the snow so completely, but when they reached it, Mac yanked the door open, handed each of them two bricks, and grabbed up two for himself.

They fought their way through the drifts and swirling snow back to Mrs. Sterling, and once more they tried to form a letter S from the green fabric.

"My hands are frozen," Jill said. "My fingers won't bend."

"Pull the top of that S into a better curve." Mac ignored Jill's complaint. "Then set a brick on it to hold it down."

Jill scowled at him, but she did as he ordered. "Hey, it's not working. I mean, the whole thing sinks into the snow."

"Set the brick on *gently*." Mac paused to watch her try again.

Tracy helped Jill pull the fabric from the snow and reshape it, putting it in a different place. Then, while Tracy held it, Jill tried to ease the brick on it. Again brick and fabric sank into the snow and snow caved in around and on top of them.

"Gang, this isn't going to work," Tracy said, after they had tried a third time and failed.

"That's negative thinking," Tom said. "Let me try." He dragged the material to a fresh spot and just as he was shaping the S, they heard the plane approaching.

"Hurry!" Mac tugged at the fabric. "Here it comes."

But they couldn't hurry. The more they tried to hurry the more they floundered and fell, dragging the draperies down with them. The plane flew over and on toward Des Moines.

"What lousy luck!" Tom exclaimed. "Why couldn't he look down?"

"And what if he had, man?" Mac asked. "We probably just looked like kids out playing. That was our chance and we blew it."

"Let's go inside," Mrs. Sterling said. "The SOS is a good idea, but it's just not going to work until the wind dies down."

"We might cut the drapery material into strips instead of trying to use it rolled in cylinders," Jill said. "The strips would be lightweight and maybe they'd stay in place."

"Let's think about it inside," Mrs. Sterling said. "No point in freezing out here any longer."

Tracy grabbed her two draperies and trudged back to the house, letting Mac go first and open a trail for all of them. They left the draperies on the porch and hurried on inside where the boys refueled the fire. Nobody spoke until they were warm again.

Later in the afternoon, Mrs. Sterling rationed out a few crackers and peaches to go along with their water and nobody refused a share. How long did it take a person to die from starvation? Tracy tried to put that thought from her mind. They would be rescued soon — if not today, then tomorrow. After they finished eating the last of the crackers, she wandered into the kitchen, wanting to be alone with her thoughts. But Mac joined her.

"Cheer up, Tracy. We'll be out of here tomorrow for sure. Just heard a weather report and it said that the winds were supposed to die down in late afternoon or early evening."

"Good."

Mac took her hand, but she pulled away.

"Come on, Tracy." Mac took her hand again. "I think we need to talk."

"There's really nothing much to talk about, is there?"

"I think there's a lot to talk about. I realize that for some reason you've had a bad time in this house — worse than the rest of us."

He was holding her cold hand between his warm ones, and she welcomed his touch. "Thanks for realizing." Her voice sounded flat even to her own ears, but she couldn't help how she felt. She had expected Mac to . . . what *had* she expected from Mac? Obviously she had expected more than he had to offer. But had she really expected too much?

"I think Tom wrote the note, Tracy."

"What makes you think so?"

"It's the kind of trick he'd play. And he's the one who would benefit from it, isn't he? He's the one who wants to write the story of our survival. I think he's trying to get all the reactions from us that he can. You've been supplying plenty of them, you know."

She caught herself just before she said, "What's *that* supposed to mean?" That was Mac's line. "And I suppose you think Tom

101

disguised himself as a girl and appeared at my bedside. I suppose you think he's the one who pushed me down the stairs."

"No, I don't believe that at all. Tom was with me when your so-called ghost appeared. And Tom was in the living room with the rest of us when you fell. All I'm blaming him for is the note. He'll confess sooner or later. You'll see. Old Motor Mouth won't be able to keep a secret for long."

"I can't explain the stuff that's happened, Mac. I wish I could, but I can't."

"Forget it, Tracy. Forget it."

"That's easy for a person to say, a person who doesn't believe Victoria was here."

"Don't start on that again." Mac sighed and let go of her hand. "I've told you how I feel."

"And when you tell me that, you also tell me how you feel about *me*."

"Not at all." Now Mac put his hands on her shoulders and turned her until she faced him. "I believe in you very much. I wouldn't have asked you to be my wife if I didn't believe in you. Tracy, people react to stress in different ways. You can't help your reactions. Once we get home, get some food and a lot of sleep, you'll forget all about this ordeal."

"I don't think so." She looked directly into Mac's eyes. "I may forget the ghost and the fall and the note, but I'll never forget that you didn't have faith in what I said." She eased Mac's hands from her shoulders and stepped away from him. "Marriages are built on faith, Mac."

· 10 ·

Tracy left Mac in the kitchen and returned to the living room, where Mrs. Sterling and Jill had pulled the rockers to the fireside. "I think I'll lie down for a while."

"Tracy!" Mrs. Sterling said. "Not upstairs! It's too cold up there. If you want to nap, why not bring a blanket down and lie on the sofa?"

Tracy hadn't been about to go upstairs, but she wanted to get away from the others, especially from Mac. She needed to be alone where she could try to think things through.

"Are you feeling all right?" Jill asked.

"Just tired." She could have added exhausted. Starved. Angry. Disappointed. Hurt. But she didn't. She wasn't a complainer.

"You've had a rough day," Jill said. "That lump on your forehead has really turned black and blue."

"I can imagine. I still ache all over."

"I'll get you a blanket." Jill hurried off,

ran up to a bedroom, and returned with a soft quilt. "Lie down and cover up."

Tracy didn't argue. She arranged one of the velvet sofa cushions for her head before she stretched out, turning her back to the fireplace as Jill covered her with the quilt. She closed her eyes. Privacy. At least it was as close as she could come to privacy in a room shared with four others.

After a few minutes she realized that she might be able to shut herself away from people by turning her back and closing her eyes, but she couldn't shut out her own thinking. Her mind was like a huge theater. The appearance of Victoria Graydon, the push down the stairs, the warning note — thoughts of all those things skulked along the catwalks of her brain while Mac's words and actions replayed on center stage.

It wasn't as if she had never had a disagreement with Mac before. They had argued sometimes about a lot of unimportant things. About what they would do on Saturday night, or about what movie they would see. They had always been able to settle minor disputes on a friendly basis. But this time it was different.

Their disagreements these past two days had concerned basic matters. She believed their love was still there, and of course that was the most basic matter of all. Or was it? Trust. Understanding. Faith. Weren't those the cornerstones on which love was built? What had happened to Mac's faith in her?

His trust? And where was his understanding? Even with her eyes closed she felt herself scowling.

On the other hand, where was her trust in him? And why didn't she have faith that he would understand her? When she looked at those concepts from his point of view as well as from hers, she could see their whole relationship going right down the tubes unless they did something to stop it. But what?

Maybe Mac was right. Maybe after they got home and had a chance to rest up from this ordeal, the happenings of these days would fall into a perspective which she could accept and live with. But that certainly didn't help her right now.

She wanted to sleep. Sleep would blot out a few minutes or a few hours of this present mess. But she couldn't quite drop off into that other world. She was too hungry. She kept hearing the crackling fire, the murmur of voices, and the incessant howl of the wind. Then suddenly after a long while she felt someone watching her. She opened her eyes and saw Jill standing at the foot of the couch.

"Hi. Thought I'd check to see if you were asleep."

"Just resting." Tracy pushed herself to a sitting position and offered Jill a seat. Mrs. Sterling was huddled beside the fire reading a book, and the boys had found a deck of cards and were playing rummy on the utility table in the kitchen.

"I want to apologize." Jill sat down beside Tracy and covered herself with part of the quilt. "I'm sorry I told the guys about your seeing the ghost girl again. I should have kept my big mouth shut."

"It's okay." Tracy was surprised to find that she meant what she had just said to Jill.

"Really?"

Tracy kept her voice low so the conversation would just be between the two of them. "I was mad at first, but I've been thinking. It's just as well that everyone found out. Mac's reaction has given me a lot to think about."

"I didn't mean to cause trouble between you two. You know that, don't you?"

"You didn't cause any trouble. It was there all the time and I just hadn't realized it. Or maybe I didn't want to realize it."

"You sound as if you and Mac are breaking up." Jill frowned.

"I hope not. No, of course we aren't. Mac's the only guy for me. I've known that for a long time. It's just that we're going to have to, well, I don't know for sure what I mean, but Mac and I are going to have to have some discussions about some really serious matters once we get home."

Jill waited and when Tracy said no more, she spoke up again. "Tracy, what I came over here to say is that I've decided to help you."

"Help me what?"

"Help you do whatever it is you plan to do

to help Victoria. What good is an apology unless I back it with some action?"

"But I don't know what I'm going to do. I haven't any plans. I guess I've been thinking so much about myself that I haven't really given Victoria much thought."

"I can see why. Her story was really strange. And spooky, too. Two deaths involved. And all that hate she felt toward her sister. It's scary."

"I've been thinking about it some, Jill, but I can't even begin to guess what might have happened to Rowena. Of course, people do drop dead of heart attacks, that's for sure. Nanny's death isn't as much of a puzzle as Rowena's."

Jill leaned toward Tracy. "Do you suppose that Rowena committed suicide and that Nanny knew it but kept quiet to prevent scandal?"

"Have you looked at that painting of Rowena?" Tracy shook her head. "She doesn't look like the suicidal type to me."

"She looks very determined and absolutely sure of herself," Jill added.

"But I suppose people can change. She might have been determined and sure when the portrait was painted and then later she might have gone into a depression. But I don't think so. Victoria was the one who was depressed. She's the one who lost the boy she loved."

"Maybe Rowena wasn't as healthy as she

appeared, not as healthy as her family believed her to be," Jill said.

Tracy shook her head. "But if she had something wrong with her, surely the doctor would have discovered it."

"Maybe she had some mysterious disease. Doctors didn't know as much a century ago as they know now."

"That's true, yet . . ."

"Yet what?" Jill asked.

"Oh, I don't know. It's just nothing, probably, but I keep thinking about Nanny's last words to Victoria."

"What were they? She just told Victoria that she, Victoria, hadn't killed Rowena by wishing her dead. Wasn't that it?"

"There was more. Nanny also said, 'In my secret journal . . .' — just those four words of a sentence she never finished. But those words make me wonder about that journal."

"A journal is sort of a diary, isn't it?"

"A place to record thoughts, impressions, and feelings. I think Nanny may have written something special in her journal. Something about Rowena that the Graydon family never learned. I wish we could find that journal."

"You've got to be kidding!" Jill looked at her as if she might have lost her mind.

"It's a far-out idea, I suppose, but I keep getting hung up on that word *secret*."

"I suppose that means Nanny kept it hidden from everyone. Nothing so special about that. I used to hide my diary from my little brother."

"Where did you hide it?"

"Under my mattress. Not a very original hiding place, but he never found it."

"Maybe that's it."

"Maybe that's what?"

"Maybe Nanny hid her journal right here in this house, Jill. It's where she lived. She died suddenly, and her journal might still be hidden here somewhere."

"After all these years? A century?"

"Why not? The journal was probably in a book of some sort. A book isn't going to disintegrate. If Nanny hid it here, it might still be here. Jill! That's what we can do to help Victoria. We can try to find that journal and see if Nanny revealed anything in it that might be of importance to Victoria."

"I suppose it could be hidden here somewhere, but a lot of people have lived here since that long-ago Graydon family."

"No, there haven't been a lot of people, Jill." Tracy lowered her voice even more, not wanting Mac to hear her or know what she was thinking. "Dad said Widow Graydon lived here for years with her spinster daughter. The mother must have been a niece or a cousin to Victoria and Rowena. And then the spinster daughter, Mary, lived here until she died twenty years ago. Dad said Mary Graydon was an old, old lady then. If just two old ladies have lived here in the past hundred years or so, a journal that was hidden might still be hidden."

"I'll help you look. At least it'll be something to do to pass the time. Where do we start?"

"Which room do you suppose Nanny lived in?"

"Weren't servants' quarters on the third floor?"

"I'm not eager to go up there again, Jill. There was nothing up there."

"But we weren't hunting for anything special when we looked," Jill said. "We might see hiding places we overlooked if we check the place out again."

"What about that pantry?" Tracy lowered her voice again. "It's big enough to have been a small bedroom and it would have been handy to the kitchen. Nanny did the cooking. At least that's what Victoria said. Maybe Widow Graydon turned the room into a pantry because she didn't have servants."

"Okay." Jill folded the quilt. "We might as well start looking in the pantry as anywhere. Let's go. But don't let on to Tom and Mac that we're searching, okay? I don't want Tom laughing at me."

"Hah! I suppose you think I want to hear Mac's laughter!"

They casually walked into the kitchen, passed Mac and Tom and their card game, and went on into the pantry where they searched the almost empty shelves that lined two of the walls. Stooping, Tracy looked on the underneath sides of the shelves to be sure a journal hadn't been taped there. Nothing. They examined a small table on the other side of the room.

"Maybe there's a secret drawer." Jill removed the center drawer which was the only one they could find. Stooping again, Tracy peeked into the opening. Nothing.

"There's nothing here," Tracy said. But she tapped gently on the walls, looking for a loose bit of plaster, a loose board.

"What's going on in there?" Mac called out.

"Nothing," Jill called back as she and Tracy examined the floor. Bare pine. And every board was nailed securely in place.

"No use checking the rooms on the second floor," Jill said. "They would have been family quarters. Rowena. Victoria. The parents. Nanny wouldn't have hidden her journal where the family might have found it."

"What you're saying is that we should check out the third floor again?" Tracy tried not to shudder at the thought.

"Not if you really don't want to. This is your search, remember? I'm just the helper. I don't blame you for not wanting to go back up there."

"You're making me feel like a real coward. I guess nothing's going to happen as long as someone else is along." Tracy fought her fear. "Let's take a quick look before sunset. I'm not going up there after dark."

"Where are you going, Tracy?" Mac asked as he saw her heading for the stairway.

"Just up to the third floor. We're going to look out the windows, check the drifts."

"I'm coming with you," Mac said.

Tracy sighed and shrugged. "Come on, then." She winked at Jill when Mac wasn't looking.

On the third floor once more they studied the huge area. The floor was solid. No hiding places there — not that she let Mac know what she was really looking for. And the rafters were exposed. She saw no place where anyone could have hidden a book. Mac had gone to the window and was looking out.

"Never saw such drifts," he said.

Once again Tracy and Jill tugged open the door at the far end of the room.

"What are you doing?" Mac said, joining them. "There's nothing in there."

Silently Tracy agreed. There were no hiding places. The room was too small to have been Nanny's quarters. She thought again that she probably lived in the pantry downstairs.

"Let's try that other door one more time," Tracy said.

They approached the door and Mac helped them, but it wouldn't budge. They grasped the latch, counted to three, and pulled one more time. This time the door opened and they almost fell down, they had been pulling so hard.

Mac peeked inside the room first and shook his head. "I told you there wouldn't be anything there. Except for this gray rag rug on the floor, it's just like the room next to it. And it's just as empty."

Tracy sniffed. "What's that funny smell?"

Mac inhaled deeply. "Smells sort of oily or something. Must be from that rug."

Tracy picked the rug up, peered beneath it, and dropped it. They were wasting their time. There were no hiding places here and she wanted to leave before Mac caught on that they were looking for something. When they got back downstairs Mac joined Tom again and Tracy led Jill aside.

"I've got an idea, Jill. A logical idea, I think. We're going to have to search the cellar."

"Yuck! I don't know . . ."

"Think about it. Who would be the one who had to go to that cellar most often? Nanny, right? She was the cook, and that cellar was where she kept the fruits and vegetables and canned stuff. The rest of the family would have had little reason to go down there."

"I suppose that's right."

"So wouldn't that be a logical place for Nanny to have hidden a journal?"

"The boys have torn out almost all the shelves. At least that's what they've been telling us. Where do you suppose a person would have hidden a journal, if not on the shelves?"

"I don't know. We'll just have to go down and take a look. Come on. Let's get a candle."

They hurried to the kitchen, found another candle, and lighted it.

"What are you doing *now?*" Mac asked.

Tracy thought fast. "We're going to the cellar to see how much firewood is left."

"Not much," Mac said. "I'll tell you that."

"We want to see for ourselves. Maybe you've overlooked some." Tracy held the candle and led the way down the dank, cold steps. Again the smell of mice assailed them and again they heard the sound of scampering feet.

"I really don't think I want to go down."

"Come on," Tracy insisted. "We haven't really searched down here at all." She almost dropped the candle as a web caught on her nose and clung there in spite of her efforts to brush it away. The musty, dank air felt so heavy she thought she might not be able to breathe. Maybe Jill was right. Maybe this was a crazy place to look for a journal. And surely the dampness would have ruined the pages by now, had Nanny hidden it here.

Tracy was just about to suggest they give up the search and go upstairs when she felt a strong draft chill the back of her neck. In the next instant the candle flame wavered, and before she could cup her hand around it to protect it, it went out.

• 11 •

"Jill?" Tracy whispered and stood motionless, unable to move. "Jill, are you here?"

"Help!" Jill shouted. "Somebody help us!"

Mac aimed the flashlight beam into the cellar. "Sorry," he called out as he hurried down the steps with a match to relight their candle. "I forgot about the draft from that kitchen door. I was just going to step outside a minute to see if the wind had died down."

Tracy smelled the sharp odor of sulphur and the more mellow fragrance of candlewax as Mac struck a match to light the candle. The flame wavered and threatened to go out again.

"You're really shaking, Tracy," Jill said. "Maybe we should go back upstairs."

"Yeah, maybe we should. I don't like it down here, that's for sure."

Jill turned and started back to the kitchen, and Mac twined his fingers through Tracy's.

"I'm really sorry, Tracy. I didn't do it on purpose."

"I know you didn't, Mac. I'm just jumpy. It's not your fault." She leaned to Mac's touch as he released her hand and slipped his arm around her waist. She had misjudged him, misjudged both of them. How could she have doubted the foundation of their love? This creepy house was doing crazy things to her thinking. Once they were back home again she would forget this ordeal of cold and hunger and fear. No. Maybe she should remember it, remember how caring Mac had been.

"Good news, kids," Mrs. Sterling said as they stepped into the kitchen. "The wind has died down enough that the maintenance crews can go into action. They'll begin snow removal immediately, working around the clock."

"Well, all right!" Tom shouted and slapped Mac on the back. "It's about time!"

"We've got to keep the fire going," Jill said. "We need to keep smoke pouring from that chimney. Sooner or later someone's going to see it and know we're here needing help."

"But we're about out of boards from those old cellar shelves." Mac pointed to a stack of lumber at the side of the hearth. "What you see is what you get. We should have been more conservative, I suppose."

"I can see the headlines now," Tom said. "RESCUE CREWS UNCOVER THE FROZEN BODIES OF FIVE CONSERVATIVES.

Negative, man, negative. After we use the shelving, we can start on the furniture."

"You're kidding!" Tracy said. "Some of this furniture is valuable. Antique, you know."

"If it's so valuable, why hasn't someone stopped by to claim it?" Tom demanded.

"It's in the Graydon estate," Tracy said. "Those cousins in California have to get together and make a decision on selling the house and contents. At least that's what Dad says. And so far they haven't done it."

"Well, I wouldn't want them to rush their decision," Mac said. "After all, only twenty years or so have passed and ..."

"I know it's crazy," Tracy said. "I guess there haven't been any eager buyers because of the ugly rumors concerning the place. But the fact remains that this furniture isn't ours. We're trespassing. We've already destroyed the draperies."

"Yeah," Tom said. "And we ate that box of crackers, too. The law will probably really be on our case for that. Tracy, wake up. We're desperate. We could freeze before rescue crews discover us. It's probably zero out there or below, and with night coming on it'll get even colder."

"Don't forget to remind us about the windchill factor," Mac said. "We'd all love to hear about that. Let's see, if it's zero and the wind is blowing at twenty miles per hour, that makes the wind-chill ..."

"Come on, you guys," Tracy said. "Stop it. I've just thought of an idea of how we can make the SOS work for us without using bricks."

"Maybe the draperies will stay in place now," Jill said. "The wind's not blowing so hard."

"It's blowing enough," Tracy said. "But with this idea, the wind won't matter."

"Okay, let's hear it," Tom said.

Mrs. Sterling nodded and looked out the window. "What is it, Tracy? If we're going to do anything, we're going to have to hurry. There may be some planes out this afternoon, but it'll be dark soon."

"We can take this old rug off the floor, arrange the letters on it, and then pour water on them to freeze them in place so they won't blow away."

"All right!" Tom slapped Tracy on the back. "Now you're really thinking!"

"But will green letters show up against the rug?" Jill asked.

"After we've frozen the letters in place we can fill in around them with snow," Tracy said. "That would make them visible."

"Let's try it," Mrs. Sterling agreed. "Boys, you roll up that rug. We'll help you lift the sofa and chair off of it."

In a matter of five minutes they had the rug spread on the north side of the yard. Tracy and Jill arranged the letters in place while Mac and Tom soaked them with water.

"We're using all our drinking water," Mrs.

Sterling said. "But I'm glad you had plenty of snow melted and ready to use."

"There's lots more where that came from," Mac said, sighing.

"As long as we have a fire, that is," Tom added.

"And I'm going to see to it that we have a fire," Mac said. "Maybe we could take boards from that old shed."

"What about using the pantry shelves?" Jill asked.

"There aren't many shelves there," Tracy said.

"Worry about it later," Tom said. "Right now, let's be sure we have these letters well in place."

"The water's freezing almost instantly." Tracy looked at the sky. "Now if a plane will just fly over! If somebody sees the message we could be rescued tonight." Her words sounded convincing enough, but Tracy was surprised to realize that she wished she would have enough time to continue searching for the secret journal. The more she thought about it, the more she was convinced that the book had to be hidden someplace in the Graydon house. They really hadn't checked in the basement as they had planned to do.

"Let's get back inside, kids," Mrs. Sterling said. "The SOS looks fine to me. There's no use standing here in the cold."

"Naw," Tom agreed. "Much more comfortable to go inside and freeze to death."

"Nobody's going to freeze to death." Mac

took Tracy's hand. "When the shelving's gone, we'll start on the furniture — least valuable pieces going first, of course."

"And who's to say what's valuable and what isn't?" Tracy asked. "Nobody here is an authority on antiques." She pulled off a mitten and blew on her fingers to warm them.

"Inside everyone!" Mrs. Sterling ordered. "We'll discuss fuel when the need arises. Inside!"

They needed no more urging. Once they were back inside everyone laid mittens on the hearth to dry, and Tracy thought the room smelled like wet sheep. The boys began melting more snow. That would be supper. Sometimes Tracy felt weak from lack of food; then at other times she forgot all about being hungry. Jill complained of a headache and so did Mrs. Sterling. The boys found the nagging hunger hard to take. Tracy tried not to think about food or home or her parents or her job. But what else was there to think about?

"The journal, that's what," she muttered to herself.

"What?" Jill asked.

Tracy felt herself blushing. Had she said it out loud? Maybe hunger *was* getting to her. She kept her voice low as she spoke. "I'm going to look for that journal on the bookshelves. Maybe it was hidden in a place so obvious that nobody would think of looking for it there."

"Dream on, sweet one. But if you find it, call me."

"I suppose it would kill you to help me look?"

"Okay. Okay. I'll help."

"Don't make a big thing of it. I don't want Mac or Tom asking questions. Right now they're busy in the pantry counting shelves."

They went to the bookshelves at one end of the living room and began a systematic search, pulling out each volume and looking inside it.

"Wouldn't just looking at the titles be good enough?" Jill asked after a while.

"No. If a person wanted to hide a journal, she might remove the regular pages from a book and insert her own pages. That would be clever hiding, don't you think?"

"Sure. Really clever."

Jill's tone told Tracy that she didn't think they were going to find anything, but they kept looking. Tracy found some of the books very interesting.

"Hey," Mac called out, stepping from the kitchen. "What are you two doing?"

Again Tracy thought fast. "Just looking at this old cookbook." Tracy held the book toward Mac and pointed to a recipe for bear stew. "Read the directions, Mac. 'First shoot a bear...' How about that!"

"Logical." Mac laughed. "No bear, no stew! But did they have bears in Iowa?"

"I think they did a long time ago. Or maybe the cooks could substitute bobcat or wolf. They had those."

"Bobcat stew?" Mac asked. "Yuck!"

Tracy continued to check the books until she found an ancient first-aid manual and medical aid. She thumbed through it idly at first, and then remembered Victoria telling her that Nanny had given her laudanum for her headaches and to soothe her mind. What was laudanum? She had never heard of it. Turning to the index, she looked under the l's. Laudanum. There. She found it.

Laudanum — a tincture of opium. Any preparation in which opium is the chief ingredient. Poisonous in large doses.

She closed the book and replaced it on the shelf. She could use a little laudanum right now herself. Her head was beginning to ache at the left temple.

Mrs. Sterling served large glasses of water for supper and they drank them by firelight. Tracy sat close to Mac, thinking that under better circumstances this could have been a romantic situation with the flickering flames lighting Mac's broad cheekbones and blue eyes, the warmth against her own face, the fragrance of the burning pine.

"I think we should plan to stay up only until this fire dies down," Mrs. Sterling said. "Then we can go to bed to keep warm."

"And let the fire go out?" Tracy asked.

Mrs. Sterling nodded. "It's dark outside. Nobody saw our SOS. We'll be here all night and maybe another day!"

"Oh, no!" Jill wailed. "Surely by tomorrow morning . . ."

"We've been saying 'surely by tomorrow' since Saturday night and this is Monday." Mrs. Sterling frowned as she looked at the boards stacked beside the hearth. "Our fuel supply is low. I don't want to burn furniture any more than Tracy does. That's going to. be a last resort. So let's really conserve tonight."

"Okay. Okay," Jill agreed. "We didn't have any fire that first night and we survived. But I'm going to bed right now while I'm still warm."

"I'm with you." Tracy rose.

"Hold it," Mac said. "I'm going outside to bring in some of those bricks — five of them. We can heat them and take them to bed with us. Why didn't we think of that sooner?"

"Good idea, man," Tom said. "I'll go with you."

In a few moments the boys were back, placing the bricks on the fireplace grate. Tracy watched the snow melt from them and listened to it sizzle as it dripped into the flames. When the bricks were hot, Tracy helped Mac wrap them in towels; then they all trooped upstairs.

"Jill," Tracy said. "Will you sleep with me tonight? I mean, I'd really like to have company."

"Sure. I don't mind as long as we're together."

Tracy and Jill crawled into bed after placing the towel-wrapped bricks at their feet. "Luxury," Tracy said, feeling the warmth on her toes. "Pure luxury."

They lay in silence for a long time, and Tracy wondered if Victoria would appear again.

"Jill? You awake?"

"Uh-huh."

"This room is spooky."

"I know."

"But you've got your eyes closed," Tracy said.

"That's what people do when they try to sleep."

"Well, open them for a sec and look at that painting. The moonlight is shining through the window and lighting it as if — well — it's almost as if she's watching us."

Tracy propped herself up on one elbow and looked at the picture. Rowena Graydon stared back at them in haughty arrogance. "She must have been a real doll. She probably gave Victoria a bad time all her life."

Tracy closed her eyes so she wouldn't have to look at the picture, but the more she thought about the Graydon sisters, the more she wished she could do something to keep her promise to Victoria.

"Jill, you still awake?"

"Yeah. Now I am."

"We never did search the cellar for that journal. Are you, I mean, how about going down there now and taking a look around?"

"Now? In the middle of the night?"

"It's not really the middle of the night. It's probably around seven o'clock."

"It's as dark as if it were the middle of the night."

"So what? It's dark down there even in the daytime and we've got candles. We could both take one. Jill, you promised me you'd help."

"Tomorrow, okay?"

"Tomorrow might be too late. We might be rescued early in the morning."

"Dreamer."

Tracy slipped from bed. "I'm going, Jill. Are you coming?" She felt guilty at the white lie. No way would she go into that cellar alone, and she didn't want Mac to know what she was up to. But she knew she would never get Jill to go with her unless she acted as if she meant business.

"Okay. Okay. Wait for me. I'm not staying in this room alone."

"Come on. I'm waiting." Now that she had Jill's support she felt a little braver. Would Mac have joined her had she asked him to? She tried not to dwell on the answer. As long as she hadn't asked him, she couldn't know for sure.

They crept down the stairs in the dark and lighted candles only when they reached the kitchen.

"Tracy, I really don't want to go down there."

"No fair backing out now. I don't *want* to go, either."

"Since we're in agreement, let's go back to bed."

"No. If we don't search down there to-night it might be too late. Come on. I'll go first." Tracy went down the steps quickly this time, dodging the webs, trying to close her ears to the sound of scampering feet. She had been down here twice before, hadn't she? It was nothing but a cellar.

"So where are we going to look?" Jill asked. "The boys have cleaned out that fruit room. No use looking there."

Tracy held her candle high. The cellar was very small. It was really just a tiny area with an adjoining fruit room. "Let's check the walls. Maybe there's a loose piece of cement somewhere. And we can search the floor. Dirt. Maybe there's a hole somewhere, a sort of secret safe."

They examined the wall directly ahead of them. Tracy felt the cold cement against her cold fingers. The whole cellar smelled of earth and dankness. She scraped and tugged at every crack in the cement; then a terrible thought stopped her.

"Jill, back a hundred years ago these walls would have been dirt just like the floor. I'll bet that the more recent Graydons added this cement as a reinforcement."

"Then we're wasting our time checking the walls."

"Yeah. Let's concentrate on the floor. We're

more apt to find a secret hole in the floor than a hiding place in the wall."

"Maybe so, but . . ."

"But what?" Tracy held the candle higher so she could see what Jill was doing.

"But I've found a loose chunk of cement, Tracy. I think I can lift it out if you'll hold my candle."

• 12 •

Tracy took Jill's candle and set it along with her own on the floor while she helped Jill examine the loose cement. The wavering light coming from below cast such grotesque shadows on Jill's face that Tracy kept her gaze on the wall. The loose section of cement was almost a perfect rectangle, and a niche had been chipped from the top side of it that allowed Tracy to insert two fingers and pull. Gray, gritty dust sifted down the side of the wall as she worked.

"Pull harder," Jill said.

"I can't get enough leverage." Tracy blew on her hands for a moment to warm them.

"Let me try." Jill eased Tracy aside and pounded around the edges of the rectangle with her fist. "That may loosen it up."

"I think that did help," Tracy said, as a small chunk of cement fell and bounced against her boot. "Good. Now we have a niche at the top and another at the bottom. Let's work together. You pull on one and I'll pull on the other."

"Watch out for your toes," Jill warned. "It may give quickly."

It didn't give quickly. They pried and pounded for several more minutes before the small slab loosened enough so that they could lift it away from the wall. They stared at the hole it left.

"Nothing." Tracy smelled the dry cement particles on her fingers and felt a grittiness in her mouth. "Nothing at all. Just more dirt."

"I'm freezing. Let's bag the search, okay?"

"At least for now," Tracy agreed. "I think that if Nanny hid her journal down here it would have been in the fruit room."

They hurried up the steps. Only a few embers remained of the fire that had blazed an hour earlier. Once they were upstairs and settled in bed again Tracy lay wide awake, cold, hungry.

"Time is running out for us, Jill."

"What do you mean? We're *sure* to be rescued tomorrow. We'll last until then. I think I must have lost ten pounds, but I've read where people can live a long time on just water."

"That's not what I mean. I know we feel as if we're starving, but I meant that we're running out of time as far as helping Victoria is concerned."

"I suppose you could come back here after

we're rescued if you feel that strongly about it."

"I don't want to come back out here. I don't think that would help. Victoria said something about Rowena's death and her nanny's death taking place a hundred years ago, as if it were only on this anniversary that she could appear to appeal to the living for help."

"If we don't help her now, do you think she may have to wander about haunting this place for another hundred years?" Jill leaned on one elbow as she faced Tracy.

The moon had risen, lighting the snow. Tracy was glad their room was only semi-dark. "Something like that, Jill. That's what people say about ghosts — that if they can't rest, they just keep wandering."

"I wish Victoria would appear again," Jill said. "Tonight. I'd probably be scared silly, but you could do the talking. Or you could call Mac and Tom and prove to them that Victoria's real."

"I don't think Mac would believe it, not even then."

"You could tell Victoria your idea about Nanny's journal; then you could ask where she thinks Nanny might have hidden it."

"She probably wouldn't know. But I'll stay awake just in case she does appear. Or maybe we can take turns." She liked the idea of someone being alert all night. "I'll stay awake awhile and then you can keep watch for an hour or so while I sleep."

"Okay." Jill peered at the luminous dial on

her watch. "It's only nine o'clock. Why don't you wake me at ten-thirty?"

"Deal." Again Tracy pulled the blankets around her shoulders as she lay staring at the ceiling, her thoughts willing Victoria to appear. But nothing happened. Her thoughts drifted to Mac. If only she could really talk to Mac about Victoria. Now and then she closed her eyes for just a few seconds to rest them, but each time she opened them the room was the same. She and Jill were its only occupants.

It was the crash along with Mac's shout that awakened both Tracy and Jill. Tracy sat up frightened, her brain sleep-fogged. Then when she got her bearings and realized she had fallen asleep in spite of her resolve to remain awake, she jumped up to see what had happened. Jill's feet hit the floor, too, and they met at the doorway into the hall where Mrs. Sterling was standing and peering into the boys' room.

"What's the matter?" Tracy ran to the boys' doorway. "What happened?" Her heart pounded. Had Victoria appeared to Mac? Had she wandered into the wrong room by mistake? Or maybe she had given up on Tracy being able to help her and thought the boys could do a better job.

"Tom fell off the balcony," Mac shouted, as he pushed Tracy and Mrs. Sterling aside and pounded down the stairs to the front door.

Tom, Tracy thought, as an icy draft wafted

up the steps. Someone had hurt Tom. There was something sinister and dangerous in this old house. Her breath came in ragged snatches as she stared after Mac and then started downstairs.

By that time Mrs. Sterling had lighted a candle and she and Jill followed Tracy, arriving at the front door just as Tom and Mac stepped back inside. Tom looked like a snowman coming to life. Snow matted his dark hair, lashes, and brows. He shook himself like a dog, sending a snow spray over everyone. Tracy felt the wet particles hit her cheeks and hands.

"What on earth happened?" Mrs. Sterling demanded.

"Are you both all right?" Tracy stepped closer to Mac after Tom stopped shaking himself.

"Tom, are you hurt?" Jill asked. "Did . . . did someone *push* you?"

"Nobody pushed me," Tom said. "And only my dignity is hurt, I guess." He gave a weak laugh.

"What were you doing on the balcony?" Tracy asked. "How did you happen to fall?"

"Were you sleepwalking?" Jill asked.

Tom took off his jacket and shook the snow from it, and brushed more snow from inside his shirt collar.

"It was my idea," Mac said. "I was sort of thinking out loud and Tom picked up on it and, well, I could see a little traffic moving on the highway. Or at least I thought I could.

It's a long way off and maybe it was all just wishful thinking."

"What's that got to do with Tom on the balcony?" Jill asked.

"It wasn't Mac's fault," Tom said. "We were both cold and hungry and we knew it was a long time until morning, so I just thought, why wait. I thought I'd have a try at signaling to someone, so I took the flashlight and stepped onto the balcony."

"We thought someone with a snowmobile might see us and rescue us tonight if they knew we were here," Mac said. "But the idea was a bummer. The balcony railing was rotted and when Tom slipped in the snow, the railing gave way and he fell."

"All the way to the ground?" Mrs. Sterling stepped closer to Tom, inspecting him for damage.

"I fell to the ground, yes, but the ground wasn't all that far away — the drifts, you know. I landed in one super-gigantic snowdrift."

"You were lucky," Jill said.

"Yeah." Tom scowled. "Real, real lucky. Now I'm wet as well as cold and it's only midnight."

"Why don't you take off those clothes and wrap up in a blanket?" Mac suggested. "Then you can get under the other blankets until morning. That shouldn't be too bad, do you think?"

"I think I don't have many choices."

Tracy was glad Tom hadn't been pushed

from the balcony, but his accident served to remind her of her own shove down the stairs. She felt uneasy again, uneasy and glad for Jill's company.

"Everyone back to bed," Mrs. Sterling said. "And no more shenanigans, please. We'll be out of here tomorrow. Hold that thought."

"We've been holding that thought for almost three days." Tom groaned. "Every time I close my eyes Colonel Sanders and Big Mac start playing tag in my mind. They're . . ."

"Spare us." Mac grabbed Tom's arm and everyone started upstairs again.

"Thought you were going to wake me at ten-thirty," Jill said, when she and Tracy were settled in bed again.

"I guess I fell asleep. All that shouting has probably sent Victoria off someplace else."

"Where else would she go? Do you suppose ghosts are afraid of humans?"

"I would guess that they might be, especially humans who shout and flounder in the snow at midnight." Tracy managed to stay awake for an hour or so, but Victoria made no appearance. Tracy wished she were braver. If she were in the room alone, surely Victoria would appear. But she wasn't all that brave. She wanted Jill with her.

Tracy slept fitfully the rest of the night, rousing with hunger pangs, then drifting to sleep again. At dawn she lay awake thinking about another idea that had popped into her mind during the night.

"Jill?"

"You don't have to whisper. I'm awake."

"Think about this furniture, Jill."

"What about it?"

"It's really not very nice. I mean, an old iron bed? A chest and dresser that don't really match? When you compare it to the neat brass bedstead in the boys' room and the walnut four-poster in your mother's room, this stuff's pretty drab."

"So the furniture is cheapsville. So what?"

"It seems to me that the furniture in here might at one time have been servants' furniture. Victoria said Rowena got the best of everything. I can't believe this was Rowena's furniture."

"Then what do you think happened to Rowena's furniture?"

"Maybe the Widow Graydon was short on cash. Maybe she had to sell it or something. And so she replaced it with this hodgepodge that had been somewhere else in the house. Nanny's room off the kitchen, maybe?"

"Could be, I suppose."

"I'm going to search this furniture, Jill. If this was Nanny's stuff, then maybe the journal is hidden right in this room somewhere."

"Hey, you girls," Mac called from downstairs. "Rise and shine. We've got a fire going for you."

"Coming!" Jill jumped from bed, rammed her feet into her boots, and combed her hair.

Tracy fought a strong desire to forget

about Victoria and join the others at the fireplace. "Aren't you going to help me search this furniture, Jill?"

"Sure thing. But later. Why don't we get warmed up first? Then we can come back up, okay?"

Only the memory of Victoria and her sad story gave Tracy the determination to continue her search. "I'm going to start looking right now, Jill."

"Suit yourself." Jill shrugged and went downstairs.

Tracy began to pull out dresser drawers, rummaging through them and looking on their bottom sides. But she found nothing special. There were four drawers of hosiery and underthings in the dresser and five drawers containing purses, scarves, and even hats in the chest. But none of the drawers contained Nanny's journal. Tracy checked the bed, looking between mattress and springs. Nothing. Opening the closet door, she peeked inside. A small, walk-in closet. It held the smell of moth-eaten wool, of dust, of disintegrating leather. She was about to close the door when she saw another small chest that had been pushed under the clothesrod and almost hidden by long dresses and robes.

She retreated into the bedroom for a moment, deeply inhaling the fresher air. Then she stepped into the closet. She knelt before the chest in order to remove the bottom drawer. It must have been someone's sewing chest, she thought, as she touched folded pieces of fabric, smooth satins, frilly laces, soft velvets. But she found no journal. Sewing notions filled the middle drawer. A rose-decorated candy box contained an assortment of buttons, and an old cigar box held half-used spools of thread in a rainbow of colors. Tracy sniffed the faint odor of tobacco. No journal there. Nor was there any indication that anything had been hidden either under the drawers or behind them.

Tracy found the top drawer filled with patterns. Some were commercially made patterns still in their yellowed envelopes, while others had been homemade, cut from brown paper. With the patterns were papers of pins, scissors, tape measures. She was looking at a pattern for a doll's dress when suddenly the closet door swished shut.

Total darkness.

She waited a moment, thinking her eyes might adjust, but they didn't.

"Jill? You're not funny. Open the door and help me look around in here."

No reply.

"Jill?"

With outstretched hands, Tracy felt her way to the closet door and groped for the knob.

There was none.

As she felt a rising panic she pushed on the door, but it didn't budge.

· 13 ·

For a moment Tracy felt safer on the inside of the closet than she thought she might feel facing whoever was waiting on the outside. Who had done this to her? Again her hope rose that it might be just a joke.

"Jill? Are you out there?" She waited in vain for a reply. "Tom? Mac?"

No answer.

Again she pounded on the door. Then she began shouting in earnest, shouting loudly enough that she could have been heard downstairs, had there not been so much noise going on there. Noise? She stopped her own shouting and pounding to listen more carefully. What was happening with the others? She could hear Mac's voice, Jill's screams, but she couldn't understand their words.

She placed her ear flat against the pine of the door and listened intently. She could hear Jill and Mac and Mrs. Sterling, but she couldn't hear Tom. Was Tom right on the other side of this door playing a sick joke on her? Tracy waited until the shouting below her stopped; then she crawled on the floor until her fingers touched the hard, cracked leather of an old shoe. Grabbing it, she stood and began pounding on the door, gratified that the shoe heel made a much louder noise than her fist had made.

"Help! Get me out of here! Help!"

She was still pounding and shouting when Jill suddenly opened the door. Now everyone stood staring in a semicircle around the closet entry until Tracy spoke.

"Someone locked me in." Her throat ached from all her shouting, and her voice sounded like a hoarse croak.

"The door wasn't locked," Mac said quietly. "All you had to do was to turn the knob."

Tracy gulped and pointed to her side of the door. "So maybe it wasn't locked, but there isn't any knob on this side. I couldn't get out. I was trying to . . ." She stopped short, not ready to admit to Mac that she was trying to find a secret journal, working on a clue given to her by a ghost.

"Go on," Tom said. "What *were* you doing in there?"

"I was just investigating the closet." Tracy knew her words sounded like lies. "Someone closed the door on me."

"Oh, come on, Tracy," Mac said. "We were all downstairs. Every one of us. There was this plane flying real low, and we all ran onto the porch and into the yard trying to attract the pilot's attention."

"I suppose you think I closed myself in the closet," Tracy said.

"I don't know what to think," Mac admitted, glancing away from her.

"Sometimes people hallucinate when they've been without food for a long period of time," Mrs. Sterling said. "That could be the answer, Tracy. Let's not speculate on how the closet door shut. Just come downstairs and get warm. The boys have set a kettle of water on the grate. We'll all have a hot drink and it'll help get us warmed up for the day."

Jill and Tom headed for the stairs, but Mac waited for Tracy and linked his arm through hers as they left the cold bedroom. Mrs. Sterling closed the closet door.

"Mac, I didn't shut myself in that closet."

"I know you don't *believe* you did." Mac urged her as they went down the steps. "Just don't think any more about it. We're going to be out of this house before long, and I'm keeping my eye on you until that time comes."

Tracy felt her pulse pounding in her fingertips as they rested in Mac's hand. She hated being so angry and frustrated. Nobody believed her. Everyone believed she was cracking up from hunger. Yet if that were true, why were none of the others showing any signs of strange behavior? Were they right about her? Was she weaker than the rest of them? She didn't know what to believe.

"Mac," she whispered as they sat alone at one side of the fireplace, "I wish you believed me." She took a sip of hot water. "When you doubt me, you make me doubt myself."

"I think you have good reason to doubt yourself," Mac said quietly. "I'm *glad* you doubt yourself. Don't you see? Your doubting shows that you're still rational and that . . ."

". . . and that maybe there's hope for me yet?" Tracy pumped sarcasm into her voice.

"Well, yes. I mean, listen, Tracy. Don't worry about these far-out things you've been thinking. Just stick with me. I'm going to look out for you every minute from now until we're rescued."

In a way Tracy resented Mac, but in another way she welcomed his willingness to be responsible for her. As long as she had Mac, she had everything she needed. Sometimes she believed in fate. Maybe fate had dropped her here in the middle of the blizzard just to show her how much she needed Mac. She eased closer to him, and he put his arm around her shoulders, warming her with his own warmth.

"Hey, guys! Listen to this!" From the other side of the fireplace Tom turned up the volume on the transistor. "This guy's talking about us."

They all leaned toward the radio as they listened to the announcer's voice.

"Early this morning Hank Mercer, piloting his private plane, spotted an SOS on the ground at the Graydon property about a half mile off highway 330. As he circled the house four people ran outside, waving and shouting. Authorities are speculating that this may be the group that is still reported missing."

"You're darn right it's us," Tom shouted at the radio. Then he slapped Mac on the back. "We've been spotted, man!"

"Quiet," Mac said. "Listen. There's more."

"We realize there were five people in the group attending the Drake University music contest, but we're going to try to talk to these people at the Graydon house, hoping they may be listening on a transistor radio.

"I've just been handed this message from Mayor Barnes who is directing our rescue units. The message is for the occupants of the Graydon house."

For a crazy moment Tracy thought about all the junk mail her family received addressed to Occupant. How little attention they paid to it. But now she was glad to be known as an occupant.

"Can you people survive another day?" the announcer asked.

"How does he expect us to answer?" Mac demanded.

"Listen," Tom said.

"If you can survive another day, please send up a continuous smoke signal from your chimney at eight o'clock. At that time you'll hear a plane flying over. However, if someone is seriously ill or injured, let us know by opening and closing the damper on the chimney to release five puffs of smoke. If someone is in need, we'll send an emergency snowmobile as soon as we can. If everybody is well, the pilot will drop a package of food for you and our emergency units will continue to give first attention to cases of extreme need."

"Where's the damper on that flue?" Tom jumped up and tried to peer up the chimney.

"We don't need it," Mac said. "We don't have an emergency."

"Tracy's hallucinating," Tom said. "I think that's an emergency."

Tracy wanted to say, "I'm not hallucinating," but she wasn't really sure whether or not that was true. "Forget the damper, Tom. I'm fine. Don't you dare signal for emergency help."

"Tracy's right," Mrs. Sterling said. "I've been listening to all the announcements about people who really are in dire straits. By comparison, life in the Graydon house is a piece of cake."

"Who's in such dire straits?" Jill asked.

"There's a little boy who was bitten by a bat and who needs rabies shots. And there's a lady who's expecting twins and who needs to get to the hospital. And there's a power outage in one section of the hospital and some patients need to be transferred to other units. You may not believe it, but we've got it good here."

"Let's build up the fire," Tracy said. "Let's keep that smoke rolling in one continuous stream."

"We're going to have to start burning the furniture," Mac said. "That's the last of the cellar shelving you see on the grate right now."

"How about using the shelves from the pantry next?" Tracy asked. "That'll save the furniture a while longer. And then there's the shed."

"But some of the furniture is going to have to go sooner or later," Mrs. Sterling said. "Face it. They're asking us to stay here another twenty-four hours. Unless they drop some firewood, we're going to be out of fuel soon."

Tracy was suddenly so caught up in her own thoughts that she hardly heard what the others were saying. They had been spotted! That was great! They were going to receive food. Food! She didn't even care what it was. It could be fried liver or boiled hominy, or any of the other things she really hated. She wouldn't even care. Food. Anything would seem like a feast. Although she was eager to get home, she was glad they would be here another day, another day in which she could try to find that missing journal.

"Tracy?"

Mrs. Sterling's tone told Tracy that she had missed something important. "What?"

"I said that when we hear the plane again,

I want everyone to run outside so the pilot will know that there are *five* of us here and that we're all okay."

"We might even make a sign of some kind," Mac said. "Just write the word Sterling on it. That would tell the pilot who we are for sure."

"What have we got to make a sign with?" Jill asked.

"I'll hunt for something," Mrs. Sterling said. "While I do that you boys start tearing out those shelves in the pantry. It's almost eight o'clock and we want that fire to be going strong when the plane flies over."

Mac and Tom went to the pantry, taking the axe and the hammer they had used in the fruit room.

"I've got an idea of how we can save some of the furniture," Tracy shouted above the noise.

"How?" Jill asked. "I'm afraid we're going to have to burn it whether we want to or not."

"Lives are more important than furniture," Mrs. Sterling added.

"Listen," Tracy said. "We can go all through the house pulling out drawers. The bottoms and the sides aren't as valuable as the fronts. We can use those parts, save the fronts. Maybe they can be rebuilt later."

"Good idea," Mrs. Sterling said. "We'll try it."

Tracy nodded toward the kitchen. "We could start in there. That old painted cupboard probably isn't as valuable as the walnut and oak pieces here and upstairs." She rushed to the cupboard and began pulling out drawers.

"Have you made the sign, Mom?"

"Can't find anything to write on."

"Hey!" Tracy pointed to a knob on the front of the cupboard. "How about this? This must be a breadboard or a chopping board." She began easing the board from its slot. "It'll be flat and smooth, and you can write on it."

"Get Tom's ballpoint," Jill said. "But you'd better hurry. It's almost eight."

Tracy struggled with the chopping board, which seemed to be swollen and stuck in its slot.

"Let me try it." Jill took hold of the knob and pulled.

"You can't do it that way. You have to sort of jiggle it, ease it from side to side. Here, let me do it. I was about to get it, I think."

Jill stood aside and Tracy began working with the board again. She pulled and eased, and then suddenly the board came out and she was so surprised and unprepared that she dropped it on her toe.

"Ow!" She hopped on her good foot, curling her injured toe inside her boot. "That board must weigh a ton," Tracy said. She pulled off her boot and began rubbing her toe to ease the pain.

"Toes hurt more when they're cold." Jill held up the board. "It's really not all that big. Won't make much of a sign."

"Hey, guys!" Mrs. Sterling stuck her head into the pantry. "Hold it a minute, will you? I think I hear the plane."

Mac and Tom stopped pounding and they all listened. Then Mac nodded. "It's a plane, all right."

"Everyone outside," Mrs. Sterling ordered. "I didn't get a sign made, but at least they'll be able to count five of us."

"Watch for the box of food." Jill grinned. "Food! My favorite thing."

Mrs. Sterling and Jill dashed outside first, followed by Tom. Mac waited for Tracy, taking her hand and urging her forward as she limped along behind him.

"What's the matter, Tracy?"

"I dropped a chopping board on my toe. I'm okay. It just hurts a little, that's all."

"What next!" Mac muttered. "I didn't realize that you're so accident-prone."

Tracy was in too much of a hurry to get outside to argue, but she knew she never had been accident-prone. In all her life she had suffered very few accidents. By the time they reached the yard the plane was circling low, and they shouted and waved to the pilot.

"Take your scarves and hats off, kids," Tracy called. "Maybe the pilot will report hair color. That might give people another clue as to who we are."

The others obeyed and they all kept waving until they saw a box falling from the plane.

"Food!" Jill shouted. "Food! Come on, guys. Let's get it."

They were peering into the sun, and Tracy tried to shade her eyes with her hand as she followed the others, floundering through the snow to the spot where they thought the box had fallen into a drift.

"It has to be right around here somewhere," Jill said.

"It just has to be," Tracy agreed. "We saw it fall. We all saw it . . . didn't we?"

· 14 ·

They searched for the box of food, kicking through snowdrifts until Tracy thought she might actually faint from exhaustion. It was terrible to know that food was so near, yet so far. What if they never found it?

"I'm not giving up until we find it," Tom said. "No way."

"What a dumb thing!" Mac kicked into a large drift, searching.

"But it'll make an interesting scene in my article about our experiences," Tom said.

"Big deal!" Tracy felt as if her stomach were rubbing on her backbone. How could Tom be thinking about writing!

"Here it is!" Jill shouted. "I've found it!"

The boys and Mrs. Sterling ran to where Jill was clawing frantically at the snow near a large cedar tree, but Tracy stayed where she was, content to watch. Mac and Tom dug into the snow with their hands until they could lift the brown box; then they all headed back to the house.

"Open it, open it." Jill chanted the words while Mac found a kitchen knife and slit the buff-colored tape and rope that held the lid shut. Tom opened the box flaps so they all could see the contents.

"Wow!" Jill smiled through tears of joy.

Tracy peered into the box. Her mouth was watering and she had to swallow rapidly. Cheese. Orange juice. Lunch meat. Pork and beans. Apples. Grapefruit. Bananas. Crackers. And a can opener. What a feast they were going to have!

"Okay, kids," Mrs. Sterling said in a no-nonsense voice. "I know we're all starving and we could finish off this whole box of food at one sitting, but we shouldn't."

"Mom! You heard the broadcast. We're going to be rescued. Let's live it up!"

"They asked us to stay another twenty-four hours. We have to make this food last for at least three meals."

"Let's get on with that first meal," Tom said. "Okay?"

Tracy helped Mrs. Sterling divide the food into three groupings; then Tracy and Mac divided the first portion five ways.

"That's fair as far as I can tell." Mac studied each portion. "If you don't like what you've got, trade with someone."

"Eat slowly," Mrs. Sterling said. "Chew each bite thoroughly. I know you're starved, but take it easy. I don't want anyone to get sick."

Tracy sat by Mac on the side of the hearth that they had begun to claim as their special place, and she thought food had never tasted so good. She sipped orange juice first, enjoying the sweetness on her tongue, the cold feel of the liquid in her throat. She held a golden, brown-flecked banana in her hand, enjoying the smell of its fragrant ripeness for a long time before she began peeling it and biting into its creamy softness.

"This is luxury, Mac. Pure luxury."

Mac grinned at her. "Stick with me, woman, and I'll see to it that you always have such luxury. What more could anyone want than a wood fire and a banana?"

"'A jug of wine, a loaf of bread'?" Tracy asked, smiling back at him.

"'And thou beside me singing in the wilderness.'" Mac looked at her tenderly. "That's how it's going to be with us, Tracy. A jug of wine, a loaf of bread, and thou. Why, we even know the same poetry."

Tracy smiled at Mac, surprised that he had remembered the lines from the *Rubáiyát* that Mrs. Brink always required her senior English students to memorize. The more she was around Mac the more she learned about him. She wondered if that was the way it was with all couples who were in love. *And thou beside me singing in the wilderness.* What more could she want from life than to be with Mac?

They sat around the fire in contentment for a long time before Mrs. Sterling reminded them that the wood supply was low again. Mac and Tom rose, went to the pantry, and began removing more shelves. Tracy helped Jill and her mother clear away the remains of their meal and wash up the few dishes they had used; then Tracy began searching for the journal once more. Her toe still hurt, but if she walked on her heel, keeping her toe off the floor, she could get around without much pain.

"Aren't you ready to give up yet?" Jill whispered as Tracy began searching the oak breakfront in the dining room.

"No." Tracy pulled out yellowed linens, tarnished flatware, hot pads. "I really feel that the journal has to be somewhere in this house. I'm going to look for it as long as we're here."

"Guess you might as well. There's not much else to do unless you're really into playing rummy or listening to Al Jolson."

"Jill?"

"What? What's the matter?"

"I want to do something, but I don't want to do it alone."

"So I'll help. What is it?"

Tracy lowered her voice. "I want to go upstairs to our room, to Rowena's room, and try to call Victoria back."

"Call her back?"

"Shhh! If anyone laughs I'll . . ."

"Sorry," Jill whispered. "But how can you call a ghost?"

"I'm not sure. I just thought I'd try. And the room where I saw her is the logical place to do it. But after all the things that have happened to me, I don't want to go up there alone."

"Now that you've eaten, I don't think any more strange things are going to happen to you."

"You really think I was having hallucinations?"

"I don't know. Maybe that's just what I prefer to think, considering the alternatives."

"More ghosts, you mean?"

"Something like that, I suppose. I just have a creepy feeling about this place — like we're not the only ones here or something."

"There's Victoria."

"*You* say there's Victoria."

"And you said you believed me." Tracy realized that Jill's faith in her story about Victoria was wavering.

"I do believe you, Tracy. At least I'm trying to behave as if I believed. That's the best I can do. But I still have this creepy feeling about the house."

"Are you saying you won't go upstairs with me?"

"I'll go. Nothing's going to happen if we're together. I'm convinced of that."

"Good. Then let's do it." Tracy peeked around the doorjamb and saw Mrs. Sterling busily helping Mac and Tom in the pantry. "Let's go now before Mac misses me and asks questions."

They hurried up the steps and entered their bedroom where Rowena stared down from her golden frame in haughty disdain. The portrait made Tracy uneasy and she turned her back to it. Now, how did one call up a ghost?

"What'll I do?" Jill asked.

"Nothing. Just don't talk to me. And don't laugh." Tracy waited until Jill sat down on the edge of the bed. Keeping her back to the portrait, Tracy walked to the old fern stand, placed her hands on it, and stared at the ceiling. She wished she didn't feel like such a fool.

"Victoria?" She let the word hang in the air for a few seconds before she spoke again. "Victoria? Where are you?"

No answer.

"Victoria, if you want me to help you, you're going to have to cooperate. We're going to have to work together on this thing."

No answer.

"This is my friend Jill with me, Victoria. Don't be afraid of her. She's going to help me and we have an idea. It concerns the secret journal you told me about. Nanny's secret journal. Can you help us find it?"

Tracy waited a long time, but nothing happened. At last Jill spoke. "It's no good. This is crazy. Maybe Victoria is afraid of daylight."

Tracy turned from the fern stand. In her heart she thought that Victoria might be afraid of Jill, but she didn't say that. She didn't want Jill to leave.

"Maybe Victoria's time was up," Tracy said.

"What do you mean?"

"You know, the anniversary, the century-ago stuff. Maybe her time for reappearing ran out. Maybe she can't come back for another hundred years."

"You're guessing. But if you actually believe she won't come back again, then we might as well forget about finding the journal. It's too late. It won't do any good to find it now."

"You just don't want to search any longer."

"We've looked everywhere there is to look. Everywhere logical, that is."

"Then maybe we can think of a few illogical places. I'm not ready to give up. Not until we leave this place."

"Hey, you girls!" Mac's deep voice called from downstairs. "We're at a point of decision. Come on down here."

"What's the big question?" Tracy asked as she and Jill headed for the steps.

"What furniture do you think we should burn first?" Mrs. Sterling asked, when they were all back in the living room again. "Tracy, since your father is in charge of the Graydon estate, maybe you should make the decision."

"And take the blame?"

155

"I didn't mean it that way. I just think you should have first say in what we do about this. The pantry shelving won't last very long."

"I've been thinking about it, Mrs. Sterling," Tracy said. "And I'm wondering about that old shed where the bricks were stacked. Maybe the boys could take boards from one side of it."

"That'll be a tough job," Mac said, "but now that I've eaten I think I can handle it."

"Yeah," Tom agreed. "Me, too. I'll help."

"Let's take a look at it," Mac said. "How about coming along, Tracy? It's your dad we're going to have to answer to."

"Sure, Mac. Let's go." Tracy tied her scarf on again, slipped her hands into her mittens, and they stepped out the back door. She squinted from the reflection of the sun against the snow and then took Mac's hand to help her keep her footing as they walked along the snow-packed path Mac and Tom had cleared to the privy.

"Hey, you're limping." Mac slowed down, turning his back to the wind.

"It's my toe. The one the chopping board landed on."

"I forgot about that." Mac helped her past a slippery place. "How did you happen to drop the board on your toe?"

"Just clumsy, I guess." Tracy laughed, then suddenly she realized why she had dropped the board. Mac's question had made

156

her think, but she wasn't ready to share her thoughts with him. Not just yet. She wasn't about to say anything that might lead to further discussion of Victoria Graydon or of any of the other strange happenings that had taken place in the old house. Did all couples have subjects that they couldn't discuss with each other? And would such subjects eventually form a wedge between them that could separate them completely?

"What's the matter?" Mac asked. "You okay?"

"I'm fine." She put her disturbing thoughts aside and concentrated on the business at hand. "Let's take a look at this shed." She began walking around the outside of the small building whose weathered boards seemed almost silvery in the bright glare from the sun. A few fragments of dull red paint clung in the crevices of the wood, and she could see rusty nail heads protruding from some of the boards.

"The west side looks the worst," she said. "Agreed."

"Yeah." Mac kicked at a loose board. "Sun and wind have really taken their toll. We could start on this west side and just remove pieces of the siding as we need them."

"I suppose it's the only thing to do under the circumstances." Tracy was glad that the decision had been made. Decisions. It seemed that her life was full of them. And all of them were so important. A decision to do a certain thing could set off a chain reaction of events that could affect people for a long time in the future.

She thought about marriage. If she married Mac, her life would go in a certain direction. If she didn't marry him, her life would go in an entirely different direction. And if she married some other person — but she couldn't even imagine such a thing as that. Decisions.

"What are you thinking?" Mac asked. "You look so serious."

"Tearing down someone else's property is a serious matter." Shouldn't about-to-be-engaged couples be able to share all their thoughts with each other? "Let's go back inside, Mac. I'm really cold."

While they warmed their fingers at the hearth, Mrs. Sterling mixed some instant cocoa that had been in the food box, and they sat around the fire enjoying the midmorning treat. When their cups were empty Tom and Mac started outside to begin removing boards from the shed.

"Think I'll go along and have a look," Mrs. Sterling said. "Maybe I can help."

"Come on." Mac stood. "It's nice to get out now and then, even if it is cold out there."

The minute the door closed behind them Tracy stood and turned to Jill. "I've got an idea. Come help me check it out, okay?"

"What now?"

"I just figured out why I dropped that chopping board."

"Clumsy?"

"Very funny." Tracy scowled. "If Mac hadn't ask why, I might never have thought it through." Tracy hurried into the kitchen. "When I was trying to pull the board out of its slot I expected it to extend the full depth of the cupboard. But instead, the board was short. It came out a lot sooner than I expected."

"So?" Jill raised an eyebrow and shrugged.

"So there's some space in that slot behind the chopping board." Tracy picked up the board and laid it on the cupboard, measuring the distance with her gaze. "Look, Jill. There's just about enough space behind that board to hide a journal."

"Come on, Tracy. Why would Nanny have hidden the journal in the kitchen? I'll bet Mrs. Graydon worked in this kitchen, too. It's unlikely that Nanny had it all to herself."

"But she may have had it to herself when she needed it. At night, after the rest of the family had retired.

"Okay. So let's stop yakking and take a look."

Tracy knelt beside the cupboard and tried to peer through the slot where the chopping board had been, but it was too dark inside to see anything. "We need the flashlight, Jill. Where do you suppose it is?"

· 15 ·

Jill found the flashlight on a rocker near the hearth and gave it to Tracy, who directed the beam into the slot from which the chopping board had been removed.

"What do you see?" Jill squatted beside Tracy, trying to peer into the slot, too.

"Nothing, yet." Tracy changed the direction of the beam and put her eye closer to the slot. Then she snapped the flashlight off. She felt her heart race as she faced Jill. "It's there! I can see it."

"Are you sure?"

"I see a black book, that's for sure. What else could it be but the secret journal?"

"How are we going to get it out?"

"There has to be a fairly easy way. Nobody would hide something she used frequently in a place that was hard to reach, would she?"

Jill didn't answer because Tracy was already on her knees in front of the cupboard, opening a lower door, reaching up and under.

"I've got it, Jill. I've got it!"

Tracy willed her hands to stop shaking as she eased the book through the opening in the inner frame of the cupboard and then held it so they both could see it. It was a thin, small, black book with gold-edged leaves. The pages were yellowed with age, brittle to the touch. A corner broke from one page as Tracy turned it, and she gasped, irritated at her carelessness.

Jill sniffed. "It smells funny. Like dry wood, or maybe it's the ink that smells so weird."

Tracy sniffed and agreed that the paper had a peculiar odor, but she wasn't interested in smells. "Look, Jill." Tracy read from the flyleaf. *"This journal is the private property of Nanny Crompton. November 1882."* Tracy gazed at the journal with awe. She had never been especially fond of history, but this book was like holding a living history lesson.

"Watch it," Jill said. "Here come the boys. Unless you plan to share this with every-one . . ."

Tracy closed the journal and slipped it in her jacket pocket. "Not just yet, Jill. It's going to be our secret for a while at least, okay?"

"Okay by me. But let's sneak away some-where and read it as soon as we can."

"Right. I can hardly wait."

Mac and Tom followed Mrs. Sterling into the kitchen. All three carried armloads of wood. Tracy and Jill stood back to let them pass through the kitchen to the hearth, where they stacked the boards.

"Looks like you brought enough to last the day," Jill said.

"I hope so." Mac dusted his hands on his gray flannels. "But right now I'm ready for lunch. How about it, Mrs. Sterling?"

Jill's mother looked at her watch. "It's only eleven fifteen, but you've been working hard. I suppose we could move lunchtime up a bit."

Tracy's heart did a dive. She was hungry, but her curiosity was at high peak. She couldn't wander away from the food to read the journal. That would make everyone suspicious immediately. Sighing, she went to the kitchen with Mrs. Sterling and helped divide the second portion of the food into five equal parts. More bananas. More orange juice. As they opened the tin of lunch meat, the enticing aroma almost made Tracy forget the journal.

"Shall we save the pork and beans for supper?" Jill asked.

"Good idea." Mrs. Sterling set the cans aside. "We can heat them tonight. I like a hot dinner."

Tracy savored the salty taste of the lunch meat and the sweetness of the orange juice, but she thought the meal would never end. And even after they finished the last cracker crumbs, everyone lingered around the fire for lack of anything else to do. But at last Mac challenged Tom to another game of rummy, and Mrs. Sterling chose another book to read. Tracy and Jill watched the card game for a while; then they made excuses to go upstairs.

"I want to see if there's any traffic moving over on the diagonal," Tracy said.

"Take care," Mac said. "Want me to come along?"

"No, that's okay. Jill will be with me."

Once they were in their room they closed the door and sat on the bed. Tracy held the journal, turning the pages slowly and carefully. The spidery handwriting in blue ink was hard to read, and at first the contents disappointed her.

"It's just poetry, looks like."

"Maybe we should start reading from the back," Jill said. "If Nanny wrote in it just before she died, then the stuff we're interested in would be at the end, wouldn't it?"

"Good thinking." Tracy opened the book from the back and turned pages until she reached the last few entries.

"Go back a little farther yet," Jill said. "We don't want to miss anything good."

"Here." Tracy pointed. "Here's Victoria's engagement mentioned." She began reading aloud. "*Today Victoria accepted Zachary's engagement ring — a beautiful pearl set in a wide band with her initials filigreed in gold on the side. I have never seen her so happy, so radiantly beautiful.*"

"Here's some more poetry," Jill said, read-

163

ing over some of the lines. "She wasn't a very good poet. Listen to this:

> *Her eyes were bright as the moon*
> *As it shines in the month of June.*
> *She is gentle as a dove.*
> *Our Victoria is in love.*"

"Yeah, that's pretty bad, all right," Tracy said. "But let's not criticize. Let me turn the page." She turned several pages that only bore accounts of Victoria's happiness with Zachary. Then the tone of the words began to change.

"Listen to this." Tracy read aloud again. "*I think Rowena is trying to spirit away Zachary's love for Victoria. She smiles at him provocatively each time he comes here to see Victoria and when Victoria's back is turned she flirts with him outrageously.*"

Suddenly Tracy noticed the strange way Jill was looking at her and tugging nervously on her ponytail. "What's the matter, Jill?"

"Victoria Graydon really did talk to you, didn't she?"

"I told you she did. You said you believed me."

"Oh, I did. I did. But I *really* believe you now. This journal is saying the very things that Victoria told you."

They turned more pages and found the account of Victoria's broken engagement, the account of Victoria's decline in both mental and physical health. Tracy turned another page and as she read she felt the hairs along her nape rise.

"Jill, look at this. It's a *confession*. Rowena didn't die of natural causes at all. Listen: *I cannot bear to see my darling Victoria waste away right before my eyes. Tonight is the night I must do it.*"

"Do what? Do what?"

Tracy turned another page and read again. "*It is done. I put the laudanum in Rowena's milk. If there was an off-taste, the pepper covered it. I smiled as I watched her drink it. She is a thief and a cheat and she deserves to die. She stole Victoria's Zachary. She stole Victoria's happiness. But now things will be different. With Rowena gone, Victoria will win Zachary back. Everyone will be happier without Rowena.*"

"Hurry," Jill said. "Turn the page."

Tracy turned the page slowly, not really wanting to read what she knew must be coming next: "*Rowena is dead. Natural causes, the doctor said. Natural causes. Victoria was near hysterics. I had expected her to grieve, but I had not expected hysterics. Why does she think she killed Rowena? I must convince her that a person cannot simply wish another dead and have it happen. Had it been true, Rowena would have dropped dead long before she did.*"

"I don't like Nanny," Jill said. "A murderess! Maybe that's why this house seems so creepy. Maybe evil from Nanny still lingers. No wonder nobody wants to buy the place. Don't read any more, okay?"

Tracy closed the journal. She already knew the rest of the story. She had heard it from Victoria herself. "I don't need to read any more of it."

"What are you going to do with this — this evidence? Do you think you can help Victoria with it?"

Tracy wished she could share the journal with Mac, yet she couldn't. Not just yet. "I'll try to help Victoria with it — someway."

"Will you show the journal to Mac?"

"I'm not sure."

"I think you should, Tracy. It would prove that the things you told us were true."

Tracy didn't answer. In her heart she felt that Mac should believe her without any proof, but she didn't say that to Jill. It was too personal a thought to share.

"What *are* you going to do about all this, Tracy?"

"I'm not sure. I need to think about it for a while. But right now I'm going to leave this journal here." She glanced around the room. "I'm going to leave it right here on this fern stand and I'm going to pull the stand over in front of Rowena's portrait."

"You think Victoria will find it there and read it for herself?"

"Who knows? She might. But right now let's get back downstairs before Mac comes up looking for me. I'm not ready to talk about this yet."

When they reached the living room they found Mrs. Sterling and the boys listening to a news broadcast on the transistor.

"If the people trapped at Graydon Place are listening, the mayor has a message for you. Your families have been notified that you are safe. The snowplows will try to get through to you early tomorrow morning."

"Tomorrow!" Tom shouted. "Tomorrow, for sure. Boy, am I ever ready!"

"Aren't we all?" Mac asked. "But it has been an adventure. I think we've all proved something to ourselves about our ability to endure a little hardship." Mac stepped to Tracy and took her hand.

"More than a little, kids," Mrs. Sterling said. "This blizzard is the worst storm to have hit the area in a hundred years. It could have spelled disaster for us if it hadn't been for this old house, and your ability to adjust to tough circumstances."

"We're not rescued yet," Jill said. "Let's not get too cocky."

They spent the rest of the afternoon playing cards, talking, even dancing. They danced to the scratchy records of Al Jolson and Frank Sinatra. Tracy had hardly been able to believe that Frank Sinatra had been singing back in the 1940s, but hearing the old records made a believer of her. She and Mac danced to tunes she had never heard before.

"Chattanooga Choo-choo." Mammy." "I'll Be Around." Dreamy tunes, some of them. Pure schmaltz. But in a way they were romantic tunes, too, and she enjoyed cuddling in Mac's arms as they kept rhythm to the music. She almost forgot that her toe still hurt. Mac could make her forget a lot of things.

When black shadows began to lengthen across the snow, they heated the cans of beans, cut wedges of cheese, and divided the crackers. Mrs. Sterling had saved enough cocoa mix for one last cup apiece.

Tracy felt a certain nostalgia she couldn't understand. There was a closeness between the five of them that she knew she would always remember. They were reaching the end of an ordeal, the start of something new and fresh. But the nostalgia was there. She sensed that the others felt it, too.

"We can let the fire burn tonight, can't we?" Mac asked. "I mean, it does keep the whole house a little warmer. Heat goes up, you know. We get a little of it upstairs."

"I think we can risk it tonight," Mrs. Sterling said. "Now that we have that shed to draw on for wood, well, even if we should have to stay here longer than . . ."

"Enough, Mom," Jill said. "We're leaving first thing in the morning. Let's not hear any negative thinking."

Mac took Tracy's hand as they trooped upstairs to the bedrooms, and after Tracy told him good night she forced herself to say to Jill what she had been lacking the courage

168

to say all afternoon. She blurted the words before she changed her mind.

"Jill, I want to sleep alone tonight, okay?"

"Why . . . why, fine, Tracy . . . if you're sure."

"I'm sure." Tracy knew her voice sounded a lot more sure than she felt.

"You think Victoria might return, right? If you're alone?"

"Maybe. It's a chance."

"Mom and I'll leave our door open. If you get scared or anything, well, give us a call."

"Thanks, Jill. I'll be okay. Don't worry." Tracy went into her bedroom and closed the door. She could change her mind. She could call Jill back. She let the candle burn for a while; then at last she snuffed it and crawled under the covers, vowing to stay awake to watch for Victoria.

For a while Tracy heard the boys laughing and joking, heard murmurs of Jill and her mother talking softly. Then the house grew silent except for the groans and creaks of the frozen timbers. Tracy stared into the darkness until her eyes burned. She was just admitting that she couldn't stay awake all night when a glow lighted her room and Victoria said her name.

"You're leaving soon, aren't you?" Victoria's voice was like muted viola tones coming from a distance.

"We're going tomorrow morning." Tracy sat up. "At least, that's what we're hoping for." She looked at Victoria's long hair, the lavender dress. Nothing about her had changed. "Where have you been? I tried to talk to you."

"I know."

"Why didn't you answer?"

"I was too sad."

"Jill and I found something to make you feel better." Tracy threw back the covers and walked to the fern stand. "We found Nanny's journal."

Tracy brought the journal to the bed and sat on the edge of the mattress with Victoria, telling her briefly just what information the journal contained. "So you see, Victoria, you had nothing to do with Rowena's death, nothing to do with Nanny's death. Just knowing should be a great relief to you."

"Yes, it is. Now I'll be able to rest. I'll be free to behave as I should, won't I?"

"Of course you will." Tracy gave the journal to Victoria. "I want you to have this, Victoria. It concerns you and it should be yours."

"No." Victoria shook her head. "I can't take it. It is of your world, not of mine. Now I have the information it concealed and that is all I need. The journal is yours. I thank you deeply for your help." Victoria smiled a radiant smile. "I'll never forget you, Tracy."

Tracy started to reply, but as she looked at Victoria, the girl disappeared. A strange sense of peacefulness touched Tracy. She laid the journal on the fern stand and started back to bed. For a moment she rested on the edge of the mattress where she had sat with Victoria. She needed to think. She needed to plan just how much of all this she was going to reveal to Mac. Any of it? All of it? Somehow it seemed like such a private thing, a thing that should be kept between herself and Jill and Victoria.

She was just starting to get under the covers again when she saw the door to her room open. She paused, expecting to see Jill or Mrs. Sterling. But there on the threshold, lighted by the shaft of moonlight streaming in through the window, stood a wiry old man, his clothes rumpled, his face unshaven, his eyes glaring. He closed the door behind him and snapped the lock.

· 16 ·

Tracy couldn't move. She felt as if her body had suddenly turned into a shell and that her bones had come loose and were bouncing around inside it. She heard a scream and it took her a moment to realize that it had come from her own throat.

"Quiet!" The man's voice rasped low and husky as he took a step toward her.

Tracy had no intention of screaming again. She hadn't intended to scream in the first place. It had just happened. Now she wanted to speak, but she couldn't. She just sat there half in bed and half out, staring at this evil-looking man. Medium build. Old — sixties or seventies. He was wearing bib overalls over a gray, plaid shirt with ragged sleeves. Even in the semidark room she could see shreds of fabric hanging from his elbows.

His face was in deep shadow and she couldn't see it. But he was bald. She could tell that.

"Who are you?" she managed to ask at last. "Who?" She had screamed, hadn't she? Why wasn't someone coming to help her? Or had she just imagined that she had screamed?

"I want that journal." The man took another step toward the bed.

"It's right th-there." Tracy nodded toward the fern stand.

"Where? Give it to me." Now he turned toward where she was looking.

"It's on the fern stand in front of the portrait." Could he see it? Why did he want the journal?

The man was reaching for the journal when someone knocked on the door. He jumped, but he grabbed the book and stuffed it inside his overall's bib.

"Tracy, are you okay?" Mac called.

"Say yes," the man ordered.

Tracy hesitated, and the man lifted his right hand. For the first time Tracy saw that he held a gun. And the barrel was aimed at her head.

"Tracy?" Mac called again. "Tracy?"

"Tell him you're okay," the man whispered.

"I'm fine, Mac." Her voice cracked and she expected the man to shoot her on the spot.

"May I come in?" Mac asked.

"Tell him no," the man whispered again.

"No." The word hung in the air unqualified.

"Tracy?" Jill's voice sounded small and scared as she rapped on the door. "Let me in, Tracy. What's going on in there? Why did you scream?"

"Get rid of her," the man said.

"I'm fine, Jill."

"Then open the door."

"I can't."

"Why?"

"I'm too cold." Suddenly Tracy knew the man was going to shoot her. They had cornered him. They were forcing him into action. But maybe she could save the others. "Why don't you go downstairs and build up the fire, Mac?"

"Tracy, have you flipped?" Mac called. "Open that door."

The doorknob rattled as someone tried it from the other side, but the man had locked it.

"Tracy, open up, please." Now Mrs. Sterling was speaking to her. "This is no time for jokes. Open the door right now."

Tracy started to make another excuse, but the man shook his head at her and she held her breath, waiting to see what would happen next. Now he was standing behind the door, flattened against the wall, his gun at the ready.

The whole bedroom shook as something crashed into the door. Tracy heard wood splinter, but the door held. Then in the next instant it crashed open, and Mac and Tom lunged into the room while Jill and Mrs.

Sterling waited in the doorway, flashing the flashlight beam into Tracy's eyes.

"Behind the door, Mac," Tracy shouted. "Duck!"

"What the . . ." Mac started to speak and then stopped as the old man stepped toward the bed.

Tracy wanted to warn the boys that the man had a gun, but before she could get the words out, Mac had tackled him and she heard the gun hit the floor. Now Jill and her mother came in, carrying the flashlight and a lighted candle.

"I've got the gun." Mac aimed the pistol at the man as Tom sat on him, but Mrs. Sterling reached for the gun.

"Let me have that before someone gets hurt."

"Ain't nobody going to get hurt, ma'am," the man grunted. "Gun ain't loaded. Never kept it loaded. Dangerous to have a loaded gun in the house."

"Who *are* you?" Mrs. Sterling demanded, flashing the light in his face.

The man blinked, then squinted. "Name's Jeb Graydon."

Tracy studied Jeb Graydon, still unable to speak. His face was seamed and wrinkled, and thick, gray eyebrows hooded his eyes. He had broad, high cheekbones, a bulbous nose, and a wide mouth.

"What are you doing *here?*" Mac bent and helped the old man to his feet, still keeping a watchful eye on him.

"I live here," he said.

"But . . . but . . ." Tom stammered. "But we thought this house was vacant."

"So you were wrong," Jeb Graydon said. "I've been living here on the sly for some time."

"Let's go downstairs," Mrs. Sterling said. "It's warmer down there and we might as well be more comfortable while you explain just what's going on here."

They trooped downstairs, Jeb leading the way with Mac close behind him, ready to pounce if it became necessary. Tracy felt a growing pride in Mac. What if he hadn't been there to break into her room? What if . . . But he had been there. He would always be there when she needed him. She sat close beside him when they gathered around the fireplace. Tom poked at the wood until the yellow flames blazed high once more.

"Mr. Graydon," Mrs. Sterling said. "I think we deserve an explanation."

"Seems to me I'm the one who deserves an explanation. Here you folks come barging into my home and all."

"This place is *supposed* to be empty." Now Tracy saw that Jeb Graydon's eyes held fear and uncertainty, so she spoke very quietly. "My father is Kent Pendelton, the lawyer handling the Graydon estate."

Jeb Graydon looked at Tracy with renewed interest. "I've heard of him, all right. Lawyers!" He spat into the fire.

"Mr. Graydon," Mrs. Sterling began again.

"It should be clear to you why we're here. We came for refuge from the storm. But you?"

The old man sighed and his shoulders slumped. "I suppose you're going to turn me in to the authorities."

"We can hardly let your presence here go unmentioned," Mrs. Sterling said. "And I think there's a law about threatening people with a gun, even an unloaded gun."

"Talk, man." Tom pulled his notepad and ballpoint from his pocket. "But remember that anything you say can be held against you."

"You some kind of a cop or something?" Jeb glared at Tom.

"No way. Just a reporter. Talk, okay?"

The old man eyed Tom's pad and pen warily, but he began talking. "I'm one of six cousins who own this old place. So you see, I'm not a complete trespasser. One sixth of the place belongs to me."

"You got an I.D.?" Tom asked.

"Hush, Tom," Mrs. Sterling said.

"I lived on the West Coast until a few months ago. Tried to manage on my social security money, but it wasn't enough. Hardly covered food. Can't work no more. Got a bad back. Worked for nigh onto seventy years before it gave out on me, though."

"How'd you get to Iowa?" Mac asked.

"Hitchhiked. I found the old home place here and just sort of settled in. Thought nobody really needed to know. The living was easy last summer. Raised a few vegetables out behind the shed, but once it turned cold . . ."

"How did you manage?" Mrs. Sterling eased closer to the fire.

"Same way you've been managing. Used the fireplace once it turned cold. So far nobody's noticed the smoke. Also had a catalytic heater. Used that sometimes. That's what I've been using these last few days while you people have been running wild over the place."

"But where were you?" Tracy demanded. "We searched the whole house."

"At first I was holed up in that third-floor storage room. Had the door locked from the inside. Thought for sure you were going to rout me out."

"But we looked in that room," Tracy said.

"Later, you did. By that time you had finished demolishing the fruit room in the cellar and I figured you wouldn't go back there, so I moved into it one night after you were all asleep. Fuel for my heater was running low and I thought it'd be warmer down there."

"And what were you eating?" Mrs. Sterling asked.

"I had grub laid in before the storm hit. I gathered it and straightened up the place once I saw you people coming. I saw you head down the road. Knew you'd get stuck. Knew you'd try to get to the house sooner or later. I had plenty of time to make myself scarce."

Nobody spoke as they all thought over the old man's words. A lot of things made sense to Tracy now, but she had some questions.

"You had it in for me right from the start, didn't you?" Tracy asked.

Jeb Graydon avoided her gaze.

"Why me, Mr. Graydon? Why me?"

"Because, because of what Victoria told you." The old man looked sheepish and he kept staring into the fire.

"You mean . . ." Mac touched Jeb's shoulder. "You mean you've seen this Victoria, too?"

Jeb nodded; then he sort of grinned. "You might say she's been my best friend of sorts. If it hadn't been for Victoria and for all the murder and ghost rumors about this old place, someone might have bought it years ago. But as long as people thought it was haunted and as long as they stayed away from it, it made a right fine place for me to hole up."

"Why did you shove me down the stairs?" Tracy demanded. "Why did you lock me in the closet? And you must have been the one who left that awful note, too."

"Yep," Jeb said. "I did all those things."

"Tracy could have been killed on those stairs," Jill said.

Jeb squirmed and rubbed the back of his neck. "I'm sorry about that. Right sorry. Didn't mean to shove her so hard."

"But, why me?" Tracy asked again.

Now Jeb looked her in the eye. "Because

179

you were the one who was so determined to find that journal and put Victoria to rest. I knew that once Victoria rested, the ghost stories would gradually die down. People forget. They even forget murder if they don't have a ghost to remind them now and then."

"So that's why you wanted the journal."

Jeb squirmed and hunched his shoulders. "I figured if I had my hands on the journal, Victoria would never see it and she'd go on haunting the place for as long as I needed to live here."

"The journal?" Mac asked. "What journal are you two talking about?"

"The journal Mr. Graydon has hidden inside the bib of his overalls," Tracy said. "*That* journal."

"Mr. Graydon?" Mrs. Sterling looked at the old man and held out her hand. "Show us the journal, please."

Reluctantly Jeb Graydon pulled out the journal and gave it to her. "There goes my cover. I suppose you're going to turn me in to the police."

"Maybe not to the police," Mrs. Sterling said. "Maybe to the welfare office, or to some agency that might be able to help you. You can't go on living here during bitter weather without proper food, without enough heat, without modern conveniences."

Tracy knew Mrs. Sterling was right. This old man had frightened her and he might have hurt her seriously, but she felt an empathy for him. He was a survivor the same as the rest of them. She knew what it was to survive in this house for a few days, but this man had survived here for weeks, months. And he had said that he hadn't meant to hurt her and that he was sorry.

"My father might be able to help you, Mr. Graydon," Tracy said. "I know he'll want to meet you. He's been wanting some Graydon to take an interest in this place for years. Maybe the two of you can work something out."

"We'll see about it when we get back to town," Mrs. Sterling said. "For now, let's all go back to bed."

"You're in my bed, ma'am." Mr. Graydon eyed Mrs. Sterling.

"Look, fellow," Mac said. "You'll have to make do with the couch for tonight. Mrs. Sterling has squatter's rights."

"Aren't we going to read the journal?" Tom asked. "It must say something mighty important to have caused so much trouble."

Tracy told the group briefly what the journal had revealed. "You can all read it for yourselves in the morning."

Tracy and Jill left the others to make the sleeping arrangements and they hurried back upstairs. Tracy told Jill about her latest visit with Victoria.

"Then she knows all about the journal?"

"Yes, she knows. She thanked me, then she left. I know I'll never see her again, Jill."

"Did she say so?"

181

"No. But it was that sort of a parting. I could feel it. I offered to give her the journal, but she said she couldn't take it, that she just needed the information that was in it."

"Yeah, I suppose the information was the big thing for her."

"I left the journal on the fern stand in case she changed her mind. That's where it was when Jeb Graydon tried to take it."

Jill walked to the fern stand, picked up something, and examined it.

"What's that?" Tracy asked.

Jill held a ring in the palm of her hand, and Tracy picked it up. It was a pearl in a gold setting with the initials VG filigreed on the band.

"It's for you, Tracy. Victoria left her ring for you."

· 17 ·

Tracy examined the ring, then she tried to slip it on. "It's so small, Jill. It won't fit any fingers on my right hand except my little finger. And it's too big for that one."

"Try the other hand. If it won't fit, maybe you can have it sized at a jeweler's."

Tracy tried the ring again, finding that it fit perfectly on the fourth finger of her left hand. She held it out for Jill to see.

"But that won't do. Everyone knows Mac is going to give you a diamond for Christmas."

"I'll wear it on this finger for right now. It will remind me of . . ."

"Of what?"

"Of a lot of things." For some reason she was unwilling to share the personal thoughts that were beginning to form in her thinking.

"Want me to sleep in here for the rest of the night?"

"If you want to. But not because I'm afraid. Jill, do you sort of feel that this house has lost its — its sinister aura?"

"Yes. Yeah, I really do. But why? Was it because of finding the journal and putting Victoria's mind at rest, or was it because of discovering Jeb Graydon and hearing his story?"

"I don't know. I guess it's something we're going to have to think about for a long time before we reach any conclusions."

Tracy slept soundly the rest of the night and in the morning everyone was huddled around the transistor listening to the news.

"A snowplow and a wrecker are on their way to the Graydon property this morning. The stranded group will be brought to city hall. It is believed that all five are in good health."

Mac snapped off the radio. "Wish we'd saved some of that food for breakfast."

"Maybe they'll have a feast prepared for us at city hall," Tom said. "Just think, gang. We're going to be celebrities."

"Oh, sure." Tracy laughed. "They'll probably have the band out to play for our arrival. And won't we look neat. We all look like ragamuffins."

"They might have the band out at that," Tom said. "Don't knock it. It would make a great ending for my article."

"Let's try shoveling a path from the house to the road," Mac said.

"Yeah," Tom agreed. "Then we could

shovel some snow from around the car. It might make our rescue speedier. The plow can't get through as long as the car's in its way."

Jill and Tom headed for the car, carrying one snow shovel, while Mac and Tracy took turns with another shovel, working on the path to the road. Mrs. Sterling and Jeb Graydon stayed inside, working at setting the house to rights.

While they were resting and catching their breath, Tracy worked up the courage to show Mac the ring Victoria had left on the fern stand. If Mac laughed she didn't know what she would do.

"A ghost ring?" Mac examined the ring, peering at it from all angles.

"That's the only way I can explain it. It certainly wasn't on the fern stand earlier. It has Victoria Graydon's initials on it. And it matches the description of the ring Nanny gave in her journal."

Mac frowned and shook his head. "It's very strange. I just can't bring myself to believe in ghosts, but maybe . . ."

Tracy felt a flood of relief. At least Mac hadn't laughed. She was satisfied to think he found the ring something to wonder about, something to make him realize that humans still don't know all there is to know about the universe.

"What are you going to do with the ring?" Mac asked at last.

"I'm going to wear it . . . always."

"On that finger?"

"Perhaps on another finger later on. But I'm going to wear it to remind me of the tragedy of Victoria's life."

"You mean the tragedy of Rowena's death?"

"Did you read the whole account in the journal?"

"Mrs. Sterling read it to us after you and Jill went to bed. It was a terrible story, a sad story."

"Yes, it was. Murder is always horrible, but the tragedy of Victoria's life happened before the murder, Mac. In fact, I think it precipitated the murder."

"You've lost me. What do you mean?"

Tracy chose her words carefully, trying not to hurt Mac with them, hoping he would understand her thinking. "I believe the real tragedy of Victoria's life was her total dependence on Zachary, her boyfriend. He was her whole life."

"I can't see how being in love can be a tragedy."

"It wasn't being in love that was the tragedy. The tragedy was that Victoria failed to develop any of her own capabilities. She allowed herself to be totally dependent on Zachary. I'm not surprised that he opted for Rowena. At least Rowena showed some spunk."

"You're trying to tell me something, aren't you?" Mac stepped back from Tracy. "You're trying to tell me you've changed your mind about me, about us?"

"No, Mac. I'm not trying to tell you that at all. But don't you see?" She hesitated, knowing what she must say, but again searching for just the right words.

Mac broke the silence. "I may be beginning to see — just a little. But I'd like to think that if you loved me, you'd want to marry me."

"I do want to marry you. And I do love you very much. But I want to be fair to both of us. I have to go on to college, Mac, to college and then to law school. It'll take a while."

"Years," Mac said with a groan.

"Mac, I want to be the best Tracy Pendelton I can be. Don't you understand? It would be unfair to both of us if I were to give up *my* goals to marry you in June."

Mac studied her for a long time. "Maybe you're right at that," he said at last. "Maybe I've been only thinking of myself, thinking of how much I want you."

"You're the only boy I've ever loved, Mac, and someday I hope we can work out a life together. But for now I have to concentrate on doing the things I must do to be a full person."

"I wouldn't want you to be less." Mac pulled her close and kissed her.

Tracy was spared from having to say more by the arrival of the huge, yellow snowplow and the red-and-white wrecker with its flashing lights. She felt as if a tight band had been released from around her chest.

The driver of the plow invited them to climb in beside him, and as Mac helped Tracy up the high step into the warm cab, she looked forward to the coming minutes. She had never ridden in a snowplow before and she knew she might never ride in one again, but she was ready to look to the future, confident that she and Mac would work out a way to travel through life together. What a way to go!